of all the

STUPID THINGS

of all the STUPID THINGS

To Ralph Ellison Library
I hope you enjoy!

ALEXANDRA DIAZ

EGMONT
USA
NEW YORK

EGMONT

We bring stories to life

First published by Egmont USA, 2010
443 Park Avenue South, Suite 806
New York, NY 10016

Copyright © Alexandra Diaz, 2010
All rights reserved

10 9 8 7 6 5 4 3 2 1

www.egmontusa.com

Library of Congress Cataloging-in-Publication Data
Diaz, Alexandra.
Of all the stupid things / Alexandra Diaz.
p. cm.
Summary: Told from their differing viewpoints, high schoolers Tara, an athlete, Whitney Blaire, a beauty, and Pinkie, a mother hen, face problems in various relationships but the most devastating occurs when Tara finds herself attracted to a girl Whitney Blaire hates.
ISBN 978-1-60684-034-4 (trade hardcover)
[1. Interpersonal relations — Fiction. 2. Family life — Fiction.
3. High schools — Fiction. 4. Schools — Fiction.
5. Lesbians — Fiction.] I. Title. PZ7.D5432Of 2009
[Fic] — dc22
2009026196

Book design by A. Castanheira

Printed in the United States of America

Para mami,

who always knew I could do it.

of all the
STUPID THINGS

PART ONE

 *Tara*

OF ALL THE STUPID THINGS HE COULD HAVE DONE, Brent Staple had to go and do that. I used to think my dad was the king of stupid things, but now I don't know who is worse.

Brent and I get to school early. He said he needed to talk with the soccer coach before anyone else got there. I don't think anything of it. We've gotten to school early before and all it means is that I run on the school track instead of around my neighborhood. It's a perfectly normal thing to do.

We start kissing as soon as he cuts the engine. Our hands are all over each other; I'm sure he's forgotten about the meeting with the coach. I think about staying in the car with him, but that's not a good idea. I had my rest day yesterday and I will feel sluggish all day if I don't run. I pull away even though I don't want to.

"Ah, baby," Brent says. "But, you're right. We both gotta go. He'll be wondering where I am." His hands drop from my waist. We gather our bags and get out of the car. I take a few steps before turning around. Even though he's walking away, the happiness I feel when I'm around him hasn't faded.

"Yo, Staple!" I call. He pauses and looks over his shoulder.

I make a point of checking him out across the parking lot. I raise my eyebrows and jerk my chin up to indicate I like what I see. It's what he normally does to me, so it's like a private joke. He bursts out laughing, smiling his great smile. That's all I wanted. Just to make him smile. I walk on but I can feel his eyes on me all the way around the corner. That makes me smile too.

I run six miles in good time: 14.8 seconds faster than what I've been doing. I'm looking for endurance more than speed for the upcoming marathon, but the two together are working out nicely. The run leaves me fresh and energetic. A quick shower and I'm ready for class.

I head to my locker to switch bags. I take down the Spanish and history textbooks from the shelf and put them in my book bag.

I look up when I hear the *click, click, click* of heels scurrying down the school hallway. I would recognize that noise anywhere. Whitney Blaire: she never wears quiet shoes. Bouncing along after her is Pinkie. Her shoes are better, but still not practical.

Flipping her bleached-blonde hair over her shoulder, Whitney Blaire speaks first. "Tara, I've got something to tell you."

"What?" My attention shifts from her to Pinkie and then back.

"Don't look at *me*." Pinkie fidgets with her bag straps. "I don't know anything. She's being secretive again."

Whitney Blaire looks around. As usual, people are looking at us. Or rather, they're looking at Whitney Blaire.

"C'mon." Whitney Blaire grabs hold of my arm and leads me to the bathroom. Pinkie follows us in and then leans against the door.

Whitney Blaire takes a deep breath. "You better sit down."

I give her a look. Where am I going to sit? We're in the school bathroom, and sitting on the toilets isn't something I'd wish upon anyone. Besides, I'm not convinced this isn't just one of Whitney Blaire's dramas.

I lean against the sinks and fold my arms.

"Hurry up, Whitney Blaire." Pinkie looks at her watch. "The bell will ring any minute."

"It's Brent," Whitney Blaire finally lets it out. "Now, I just heard this, and I don't think it's true, but I thought you should know what's going around. . . ."

My fingers tap against the sink.

Whitney Blaire licks her lips and sighs. "Well, someone just told me that he caught Brent getting it on with one of the cheerleaders."

Pinkie gasps. I swallow hard. My hands clutch into fists, my fingers digging into my palm. My eyes stay on Whitney Blaire. I don't blink.

Whitney Blaire puts a hand on my shoulder. I stop breathing. I know she's not done. There's something worse yet to come. But I don't know what can be worse.

Whitney Blaire continues, "One of the guy cheerleaders."

My legs give out from under me. I slide down until I'm sitting on the floor with my back against the sinks.

Pinkie looks at both of us with wide eyes. "Wait . . . you mean, Brent and another guy were . . . you know . . . doing . . . doing *it*?"

Whitney Blaire nods. Pinkie pales and then quickly leaves her post by the door to dash into a stall. The bell rings. I still can't move.

"It's probably nothing," Whitney Blaire goes on. "But I swear, I'll find out for sure. I bet he and Chris Sanchez were goofing off and Andre's dirty mind took over. You know how boys are. They're always making sick jokes like that. Besides, Brent's not the type to go off with a guy—he likes girls too much. He wouldn't do that to you."

She waves her arms as she tries to convince me it's some crazy rumor, but I don't really see her. I just stay blank. She kicks my water bottle against the wall by accident. It rolls back to me unbroken. I hold it in my hand and squeeze it. Squeeze, release. Squeeze, release. It's the only part of me capable of moving. And I certainly can't speak.

Pinkie comes out of the stall smelling very minty. She sits down next to me and puts her arm around me. She rambles on about something random. Maybe she's talking about Brent. I don't know. I can make out words, but I can't put them together to understand what she is saying. She hands me a candy bar, something with loads of chocolate, caramel, nuts, and 273 calories in two ounces. I eat it all.

By then a teacher finds us and tells us off for not being in class. The girls help me up and gather our bags.

Pinkie says something and then looks at me for a response.

I don't know what she said. I shake my head. "I've got to run."

I take off down the hall, away from my friends, away from school, away from Brent and what he might have done. I don't care that I haven't stretched and warmed up. I don't care about overexerting myself with two runs in one day. I don't care that the candy bar is doing somersaults in my stomach. I just keep running.

Whitney Blaire

"TARA," PINK SHOUTS, BUT HER VOICE DOESN'T COME OUT louder than a whisper. "Tara, come back."

"Pink," I say to her. "She's gone."

"We have to find her. She could get hurt. She might not look both ways while crossing the street. She could trip and fall and the cars might not see her. What if—?"

She jumps when my phone starts ringing. "Answer it quick," she says, darting glances across the empty hall.

"Yeah?" I say while Pink scolds me for having the phone on during school. But at the same time she's staring at me with huge brown eyes, dying to know who's calling.

"Hey, it's Andre. You know that thing I mentioned to you earlier? Well, just forget it, 'kay? 'Cause it never happened. You didn't tell anyone, did you?"

"Tell anyone what?" I ask innocently.

He breathes a sigh of relief on the other side of the phone. "Great. That's awesome. Thanks, man." And he hangs up before I can say anything else.

I twirl the phone in my hand for a few seconds before throwing it in my bag. I run my fingers through my hair a couple times. Pink is twitching, almost ready to burst. I decide not to string her along, though it would have been fun any other time. "Turns out it was a mix-up. There wasn't anything with Brent after all."

"Well, that's good," Pink breathes, and then pales again. "But what about Tara? You shouldn't have said anything without—"

"I know," I snap, and then sigh. Crap.

I shake my head. I can't deal with this right now. I look around for a distraction.

Behind the doors teachers are doing their thing. And we're out here in the hall where they can't get to us. Even the teacher that caught us in the bathroom can't get us; by the sounds she's making, she'll be in there a long time. I grin. We can do anything. Go anywhere. And no one can stop us.

I start walking. "Well, come on, Pink. Let's get out of here. Let's go find Tara!"

We start heading for the door when Pink suddenly stops. "But wait, we can't. We have classes. I have homework to hand in."

I take her hand and keep walking. "It's for Tara. Don't tell me that a couple math problems are more important than her safety. Tara's freaked—she might end up doing something stupid."

That gets Pink moving faster. "You're right. We have to find her. But for goodness sake, Whitney Blaire, do your shoes have to make so much noise?"

Pinkie

I DON'T SEE TARA ANYWHERE. THERE ARE TWO WAYS SHE could have gone: to the right, toward the highway, or to the left, toward town. I still don't know if the idea to go look for her is a good one. The bell goes off, marking the end of first period. I've never missed school before. I should be heading to physics. I haven't been doing very well in that class; I only got 89% on the last quiz.

Whitney Blaire is half pulling, half dragging me through the parking lot. I'm out of breath. I think there's something in my shoe. And I'm carrying my forty-ton schoolbag, and Tara's bag as well.

"Hurry up, we have to get her," Whitney Blaire urges me.

"I can't," I gasp. "We have to go back. I'll just give her a call."

Whitney Blaire keeps pulling me. "She won't be home for ages. It takes forever to get to her house, no matter how fast she runs."

Of course she's right. Tara's house is eleven miles from school driving on the highway, and nine miles going through town. She only left ten minutes ago. And we don't even know if she's running home. I glance over at the school, hoping that no one sees me playing hooky. That would not look good on the college applications.

We get to my car. She starts up with a moan but then quiets down as I drive her out of the parking lot. "Which way?"

Whitney Blaire waves her manicured hand. "Highway, it's faster."

I can see the cars speeding down the highway in the distance. "But Tara's not going to run on the highway. It's too dangerous."

"Right."

"But then again, Tara's not thinking straight. She might have gone for the highway instead."

"Then we'll go that way."

"But." I stop. I have no idea which way Tara would have gone.

Whitney Blaire suddenly points. "Over there, I think I see her."

The car sways a bit from turning so sharply. Breathe, Pinkie, breathe. "Where? Where did she go? I don't see her."

"Faster. Up there—turn right and then right again."

I clench the wheel and follow her instructions. Eventually we get on the highway, but going the opposite direction from Tara's house. "Are you sure this is the right way?"

Whitney Blaire shifts her long legs so her knees are up against the dashboard. I don't know if she's paying attention to where we're going. She seems a bit distracted, but then again she always looks that way when her blue eyes are covered by her huge movie-star sunglasses. "Trust me. You just don't have a good sense of direction."

She's right of course; I've been known to get lost going home on dark nights. I shift into fifth gear. I hand her my phone and have her try Tara's house. Whitney Blaire keeps telling me where to go, but with every minute that we don't see Tara, my heart beats faster.

I can't help it. I've been worrying about the girls since I met them back in first grade. Whitney Blaire was stuck in a tree and Tara went up to rescue her. Even though I didn't know them, I was certain they were both going to die. They came down with nothing more than a few scratches, and yet it was enough for me to realize that I never wanted to lose either one. But now Tara's gone off, and I don't know if she's okay. Please be okay, please.

Whitney Blaire suddenly sits up and lowers her glasses. "Oh wait, I think we were supposed to take that last turn."

"Are you really sure?" I wipe the sweat from my forehead. "I mean, we're in a car. We should have caught up with Tara by now. Do you even know where we are?"

She pushes her glasses back up. "Course I do. You shouldn't worry so much."

I grumble and grip the steering wheel tighter.

"No, really." Whitney Blaire turns to look at me. "Do you know how pretty you could be if you'd lay off the worrying? You look like a thirty-five-year-old housewife."

I ignore her and glance at the clock. An hour and twenty-three minutes have gone by since we left school. And still no Tara. Whitney Blaire tells me to turn a couple more times and we end up in front of a roller coaster in some unknown town.

"Awesome!" Whitney Blaire suddenly perks up. "Have I got an amazing sense of direction or what?"

"Great, Whitney Blaire, except that you were supposed to lead us to Tara!" I grab my phone and quickly call Tara's house again. If she's not there by now, I don't know who I'll never forgive: Whitney Blaire for getting us lost, or myself for letting us get lost.

Tara answers on the fourth ring.

"Oh my God, Tara. Are you all right, are you okay? We've been looking all over for you. Did you get Whitney Blaire's messages? It was all a mix-up with Brent. We're so sorry. We didn't mean to upset you. Are you okay?"

"I'm fine."

I switch the phone to my other ear. "Oh, Tara, you sound horrible. This is all so horrible. Is there anything we can do? Do you want us to come over? We'll be there, don't worry. It might take a while, but we'll be there. We'll be right there."

"I'm fine."

I motion to Whitney Blaire. "Pull out that map in the glove compartment and find out where we are. Tara, you just hold on, we'll be there soon. You're going to be okay."

"I'm fine, really."

"Tara, you're—"

"Pinkie, look. I'm fine. But I just ran about twenty miles today. I am very tired. You don't need to come. I need to rest for a few hours. Really, that's all."

I frown, not sure what she means. "So you don't want us to come over?"

"I'm fine. I just want to get some sleep."

"Okay, Tara." I sigh. "If you say so. But please, please, please call me when you get up."

"Fine." And she hangs up.

I sigh again. Now that I know Tara's okay, I start thinking about school again. We're getting our Spanish papers back today and I know that I used *ser* instead of *estar* at least twice. Then in English lit, Ms. Jamison is handing out the next Shakespeare play we have to read (or in my case reread), and Nash said we might meet at lunch for a special talk about college applications for next year. I could be missing out on some very important classes that will affect the rest of my life, but I'll never know because I've ended up on some wild-goose chase.

I look at Whitney Blaire to scold her. The sunglasses are off, the distracted look is gone, and she's grinning. "So she's okay, right?"

I shake my head. "That's what she says, but—" I notice her grin is bigger and more mischievous than ever. "What?"

"David just sent a text wondering where we are," she says, but I know that's not why she's grinning. Nonetheless, I check the phone still in my hand and sure enough I also have a message from him.

Unable to hold the suspense any longer, Whitney Blaire finally lets me in on her plot. "I figured since Tara's okay and, knowing her, probably wants to be alone anyway, and since we're already here . . . well, I told David we're checking out a roller coaster!"

My stomach turns just thinking about it, but Whitney Blaire is already out of the car and walking across the parking lot. I can't just leave her here. I don't know where we are.

I let out a third sigh. "Fine."

 *Tara*

I HIT THE WALL A COUPLE BLOCKS FROM HOME. I HAVE to walk the rest of the way. Or more like drag my corpse. I can barely see. My head is light from dehydration. My thighs burn. My lungs ache against my sides. I don't know how far I ran. Ten, maybe twelve miles, in addition to the six earlier. I took the back roads by the railroad tracks that I don't know very well; it kept my mind focused on where I was running instead of why.

Last time I ran so hard was when Dad left five and a half years ago. But even that was completely different from now; I had been running after him.

Our mutt Sherman bursts out of the house. I go in but leave the door open for him. The phone is ringing. Automatically, I pick it up. It's Pinkie. She says that Brent didn't do it after all and then asks fifty times if I'm okay. I say yes I am, and no, I don't want her and Whitney Blaire to come over. I finally tell her I need to get some rest. Then I promise her something before hanging up.

I concentrate hard on getting myself back into form, stretching and drinking small sips of water. Taking deep breaths. Trying to get back in control.

Mix-up or not, the thought is still in my head. What if Brent cheated on me? With a guy.

Sherman comes over and whimpers. I place a hand on his head and crouch down. He licks my face. My breathing is returning to normal. My heart has decided not to give up. But there's a stitch near my appendix that still hasn't gone away. I rub it with one hand. I stop drinking but continue petting Sherman.

Part of me wishes I were still running. Then I wouldn't need to think. But I can't move my legs, so the thoughts pour in: Brent with Sanchez. Sanchez with Brent. Not true, I remind myself. Not true. But I need to know for sure.

That's why I answer Brent's soft knock on the door at five thirty the next morning. I need to hear it directly from him before I can believe it isn't true.

"Hey," Brent says. He leans over for a kiss but I duck away and break into a run. My body is still recovering from yesterday's exertion. I set the pace somewhere between slow and moderate. Brent is at my side in moments. Silently, we run the first couple of miles. As we get to the park, I slow down automatically. Brent and I always take a break in the park. But today we're not going to spend the time with our hands all over each other.

Not that Brent doesn't try. He places a hand on my waist once we stop. I push it away. He tries to hold my hand and I move out of his grasp.

"Baby, talk to me," he says. "What's bugging you?"

I sit down. The grass is wet with dew, but I don't care. I pull up handfuls and heap the blades in a pile. When I speak, I cringe at the name. "Chris Sanchez."

"I don't know what you're talking about." Brent kneels down and tries again to take my hand. Again I pull it away. Brent's lips press together.

I run my fingers through the grass. Deep breath. "Did you screw him?"

"What?" Brent chokes. He gets back on his feet and paces as his breaths come out in gasps. "How—what—who told you this?"

I look away. "Just something I heard around."

He swears under his breath. I watch him continue pacing, his hands on his head holding his hair.

I press against the ground and control my breathing. "So, is it true?"

He stops and looks at me sitting on the grass. I watch his face. For a split second it looks angry, but then I realize it's probably more shock and hurt. "No, baby, no. Course not."

I take a deep breath. And another. I keep quiet as I breathe. I want to believe him. I want to trust him. He's never given me a reason not to trust him. But the images are running around my head. Brent smiling at Sanchez. His hands on Sanchez. His lips . . . Brent with Sanchez; Sanchez with Brent.

I want them to stop. They have to stop. But every time I look at Brent, they come back. Uninvited. I have to move; it's the only thing that keeps the images at bay. The only way to stay in control.

Before I can sprint off, Brent wraps me in his arms.

I push him away. "Don't touch me."

He holds tighter.

I jerk to break free. "I mean it, let me go."

Brent sighs and drops his arms.

Brushing my hands against my arms, I try to wipe away Brent's touch. The images of his hands on Sanchez haven't stopped. I pace. Back and forth. I hold my head. Any minute now the images are going to take over and I'm going to lose control. I can't let that happen. Focus. But I can't.

"I can't," I gasp.

Brent leans closer. "Can't what?"

"I can't be with you." The words almost choke me as they come out. I don't believe I'm saying it. He's my first real boyfriend and has been everything I've needed. He's supported me in so many ways. But now . . . I keep pacing.

His eyes widen and his mouth drops. "Are you breaking up with me?"

I inhale deeply and exhale slowly, squeezing my diaphragm to release the last bit of air. Then I take a normal breath. "Yes."

He blinks. If I had kicked him in the balls, he couldn't have looked more hurt. Or surprised. I turn away. I pick up my water bottle from the grass and squeeze it like I did yesterday. Squeeze, release. Squeeze, release.

He puts a hand on my shoulder. It sends a shiver down my spine. But I can't tell if it's a good shiver or bad shiver. And even if it's a good shiver, I don't know what that means.

"You can't be serious. I love you," he says.

I make the mistake of looking at him. There's a sad puppy-dog look in his green eyes. He shallows and sniffs. "Tara, please."

That does it more than the three words he had said before, even more than the tortured look on his face. Brent never calls me by my name.

The images of him and Sanchez fade a bit. But only a bit.

I lick my lips. "I need some space. A little bit of space. Away from you, away from . . . this."

He sighs and then kisses me lightly on the lips. I don't respond, but I don't wipe my mouth clean either. "Okay, if that's what it takes for you to trust me. And once you do, it's you and me again?"

"It's getting late. We have to go."

He squeezes my hand before we start running again. Slowly first, and then as the images clear I pick up the pace. I know he thinks I didn't really mean what I said. But I do. I need these thoughts out of my head. And until they are, I can't be with him. As much as I might want to be.

Then comes the little voice inside my head. It asks why I didn't just finish things off completely if there's doubt about Brent's honesty. Because I love him, I tell the voice. Oh right, says the voice, and it shuts up and goes away.

Whitney Blaire

DAVID'S WAITING FOR ME BY THE SWING SET JUST LIKE I asked him to. And he's holding the history notes that I missed from yesterday. He's such a good boy.

"Aw, thanks." I give him a quick hug. "You're such a sweetie. I'd be totally lost without these."

David looks down while I rustle his blond bowl cut. He shifts from one foot to the other and kicks some gravel. He's blushing like he's ten, it's so cute.

"It's nothing, really," he says.

I shove the notes in my purse and spot a magazine. "Hey, check this out. There's this article in here that talks about the ten most important traits to have in the perfect guy. I got it for Tara, so hopefully she won't end things with Brent."

I feel kind of bad about yesterday. I acted too quickly. I shouldn't have rushed to Tara with the news. Not when it was so obviously not true, not possible, not even likely. But at the time I thought she had the right to know if she was being two-timed. I figured it was better to hear it from me than through the grapevine. That's what real friends do.

David grumbles. "What's Tara see in him anyway?"

"Oh, come on." I glare at David. "Brent's the hottest guy outside Hollywood. Any girl at school would give her right arm to be seen with him."

"Then why haven't you gone for him?"

I give him a shocked look. "A girl never goes for a friend's guy. Never ever. That's the ultimate betrayal."

He crosses his arms but keeps staring at the ground. "But you basically said you wanted him."

"David," I try to explain things to him. "There's nothing wrong with looking at something you're not going to buy."

David snorts. "Yeah, but what's going to keep you from trying it on for size?"

I don't need to defend myself. He's a guy. He doesn't know anything about shopping. Or guys. Instead, I squint at him and tilt my head. "Are you jealous?"

"No," he says too quickly. "I just think you girls should know better than to go for guys like Brent. He just uses girls to get laid."

I wave David away. He is jealous. And intimidated that Brent could have any girl he wants. Not that David should be. I missed my chance with Brent. Or rather he never offered me a chance. And now, because of his history with Tara, if he did ask, I would have to turn him down. Which, thinking about it, really wouldn't be too bad. Because that would mean I'd be the one girl he'd want but couldn't have.

I fantasize about that while David picks a handful of

pebbles and as if he's on a lake; he starts skipping them across the playground.

It's a few minutes before he speaks. "So, let's hear it."

"Hear what?" I was just getting to the part in my fantasy where Brent was sending me flowers and begging me to give him a chance. David is still focusing on throwing stones but his back is a bit hunched over.

"The ten things you need for a perfect guy."

I grin. That's why I mentioned it in the first place. David will never be anything more than a friend, but there's no harm in letting him know how he ranks.

Sitting down on the merry-go-round, I start off. "'Rule one: Be sensitive and supportive of a woman's needs.'"

David stops for a second and turns around. "I always give you a hug when I see you, and I brought you those history notes."

I roll my eyes. Boys. "History notes are not exactly what I have in mind, but I guess it's a start. 'Rule two: Don't be afraid to ask her what she wants.'"

"Do you want the history notes?"

I give him a confused look. "Yeah?"

He smiles, straightens up, and skips another rock. "Great. So let's move on to rule three."

Stupid, I walked right into that one, but I'll get him back. I stretch out on the merry-go-round. I don't have to peek to know I'm showing off some good cleavage. I scoot up just a bit. "Ha, now here you're slacking. Pink would love this rule: 'Always return a woman's phone, e-mail, or text messages.'"

David's eyes shift down and then up again. "Slacking? When was the last time I didn't get back to you?"

I have him now. "I send you e-mails all the time."

"Forwards that say 'you must send this to twenty people in five minutes or face a horrible death' are not e-mails."

"Well, you could at least send me a note to let me know you got them. Or send me forwards once in a while," I point out.

David does nothing to help his looks by making a gross face. "You like getting all that trash?"

"Of course. And it's not all junk. Some of those forwards are really funny and interesting. Don't you read them? And it's great opening my mail and seeing loads of new messages. That way I know people are at least thinking of me."

David drops the rocks left in his hand to look at me all serious. "I don't need forwards to think about you. But if it takes a stupid forward to know you're thinking of me, then send me all you want."

I laugh. I guess I shouldn't tell him that I don't know half the people in my address book; that I just plug them all in when I send forwards.

"All right, I'll let you off that one too," I say with mock annoyance. "After all, you do reply when you need to. 'Rule four: Make sure to get along with the woman's parents and friends.'"

David thinks about this one for a second. "You know, I can't remember the last time I saw your mom. And have I even met your dad? Seriously, other than being years older than most parents, I can't remember what they look like."

"Lucky you," I mumble.

"What?"

"Nothing," I say quickly. "Parents aren't important. You know and like my friends. I mean, Pink's practically your sister, so you've got that rule covered."

"Cool. What's next?"

I read out the remaining questions and we conclude that he scores eight out of ten. Well, he says he got a perfect score since the two he missed don't apply—they were about being good in bed. I stay firm on giving him an eight out of ten score. David then says the typical guy thing. "So, let's see if I can win those extra two points."

I flick my hair over my shoulders. "In your dreams."

David shrugs. "Why not? I mean, you're not seeing anyone and I got everything else right. Aren't these all the things you want in a perfect guy?"

"Sure, but he also has to be good looking with lots of money," I answer quickly.

"Ah, money," David pats his pockets. "I'll have to work on that one. But for now, you want to grab an ice cream before we start our homework?"

I stuff the magazine in my bag. It wasn't a very good article after all. It forgot to list rule eleven: always offer to take a woman out for a treat. Even though David says he doesn't have much, he never seems to mind spending what he has.

Now if only he could look a bit more like Brent.

 *Pinkie*

I GET TO THE CLASSROOM EARLY. A FEW TIMES A month, the school's Honor Society gets together. Sometimes we discuss important things like what colleges want to see on applications and developing good study habits. But we also attend lectures and volunteer in the community. Once a year we have dinner with the mayor, and at the end of the year, if there is still money left in the budget, we have a field trip to the city and go to a couple museums. It's lots of fun. Really.

I start rearranging the desks so that we're in a circle. That's how Nash likes them. He likes everyone to be able to see everyone else. Nash is really smart that way. Well, he's brilliant in all ways. He knows everything about everything, speaks something like five languages (his voice-mail message is always in a combination of English and some other language), and can do advanced math in his head. Rumor has it that he deferred from Harvard until he has saved up enough money to go. That's why he's here, being our advisor, while the rest of the time he bartends at this really expensive restaurant Whitney Blaire's parents go to. He's amazing.

"Hey Pinkie, thanks for setting things up." Nash comes in and gives me a big hug. I beam and hug him back. The world would be much better if more people hugged.

"We've got some interesting stuff to go over," he continues as he sets down his things. "I hope we have a good turnout."

"I talked with a few girls and they're way excited about coming," I tell him, and then instantly wish I had kept my mouth shut. Do I always sound so stupid? Quick, say something clever and funny and mind-blowing. "Did you know that rats get turned on by marijuana, while small doses of radiation do it for earthworms?"

Nash laughs and I blush even more. Where did that come from? Stupid, stupid Pinkie. I might as well tape my mouth shut for all the good it does for me. I fuss with the desks as people start to arrive. Nash hugs the girls and gives the guys a half-hug pat on the back. One boy, Andre, comes in with a black eye. Nash tries to hug him properly, but Andre pushes him away, saying he's fine and that it was just a stupid soccer injury. Nash sighs and then sits on top of one of the desks.

"All right, let's get started."

I already have paper and a pen out to start scribbling away. Once in a while I sneak glances up at Nash. Whitney Blaire says he's funny looking, Tara thinks there's nothing special about him, and okay, I admit it, he's not a heartthrob. He's got this messy, dark brown hair like he just rolled out of bed, and a big nose that looks out of place in his narrow face. But he wears these tortoiseshell glasses that make him look really cute in a geeky kind of way, and his brown eyes are always shining from behind the glasses. His cheeks have a perpetual five-o'clock shadow. As he talks to us, I wonder if his face feels prickly or smooth. It looks smooth.

He catches me looking at him and one of his eyes closes. I look away quickly. I can feel my face turning red. Was that a twitch or a wink? It had to be a twitch because he's not allowed to wink at students. I know there's some regulation against that. But on the other hand, he's only an advisor to an after-school group; it's not like he's a teacher. And he's only twenty-one, he's practically one of us. But still, it was probably only a twitch.

I look up at him. He's smiling at me. No, he's smiling at everyone. I must have imagined the wink. Wait, now he's definitely smiling at me. Maybe he knows I like him and finds it amusing. Oh great, he must think I'm some kind of silly teenybopper little girl. I must pretend that I'm cool and indifferent. No, forget that, or I'll say something worse than horny earthworms.

He passes around some leaflets about the most common mistakes done on personal essays and his hand clearly brushes mine. I look up at him and see it again. A wink. Even I can't tell myself it was just a twitch this time. But what does it mean? I look around at the others in the group. David is twirling a pencil across his knuckles like he's bored. Some others are doodling or sending text messages. No one noticed Nash winking.

"So, I thought I'd let you know," he says. "There's a lecture at seven o'clock tomorrow tonight at the civic center on Emerging Democracy in Islamic Countries. Dr. Wang Hall is brilliant and I have been looking forward to hearing him speak for a long time. If you're not doing anything, I recommend you go. If anything, just to get a new perspective."

Everyone kind of shrugs and starts getting their things together. David pauses to wait for me but I tell him to go ahead. I take my time putting my notebook in my bag. I check to make sure I have my phone, my keys, my wallet, my breath strips, and then I double-check to make sure they're still there. It's only once I'm certain I have everything that I head to the door.

Nash walks over and hugs me like he did the others. "So, are you coming to hear Dr. Wang Hall tomorrow?"

"Definitely," I say, even though I hadn't thought much of it before. But what if that sounded overeager? I have to say something else. I don't want him to think I'm boring and have no life. "Well, that is if I get all my homework done in time."

Nash grins. "Well, I hope you can make it."

"Me too." I smile back. We stay there looking at each other, not sure what to say or do. I move a strand of hair out of my face and then fumble to get my bag. "Right, so, see you later." I give him a half wave and get myself out of the room before I start acting very much more stupider.

Tara

MY TIMES HAVE BEEN OFF THESE LAST FEW DAYS. MAYBE because I'm still recovering from the twenty-mile exertion earlier this week. I decide to take a day off running and go to the gym to use the pool instead. The gym is like a second home for me. Mom teaches a yoga class there every Saturday on top of her regular job. It doesn't pay much but it gets us into the gym free. I only need to wave at the guys at the front desk as I walk by.

Like some magnetic force, my eyes land on Brent as he heads to the RTC, the Resistance Training Center. Through the glass surrounding the room, I watch him jerk his chin up and smile at Lola, the fifty-something-year-old with green hair working behind the counter. She rolls her eyes at him and with her stale cigarette breath comments that if only she were thirty years younger. I'm too far away to actually hear Lola say this, but that's what she told him when I first met Brent six months ago.

I was on the treadmill that day when he walked into the

RTC. Although my back was to him, I could see him clearly in the mirror in front of me. I knew him vaguely from school, but then again it was hard not to.

I remember my surprise when he opened the door for some Down syndrome kids. Instead of averting his eyes to not look at them, Brent held out his hand and high-fived each one that passed by. One little girl with thick glasses couldn't coordinate her hand well enough to slap Brent's. He bent down and held his hand just a couple inches from hers. She slapped it hard. Brent held out his other hand. She slapped again, and he gave her a thumbs-up.

He straightened up to find Lola watching him with a pen in her mouth. Slowly she turned back to her magazine and spoke to him as if he were looking at her from the glossy pages.

"What is it with you and women, Staple?" she demanded.

Brent blushed and shrugged away her comment. "I don't know what you're talking about. They're good kids, that's all."

Lola snorted and flicked over to the next page.

Half amused, Brent shook his head as he took off his windbreaker and straightened his tight white T-shirt.

I reduced my speed.

Lola, eyes still on the magazine, took the pen out of her mouth and shook it at him. "You better watch it, young man. If I wasn't thirty years too old for you . . ."

Brent laughed embarrassedly. "I don't believe you're thirty years older than me, Lola."

Lola huffed. "See, there you go again, you charmer you. But you're right. It's more like thirty-five, but what's five years?"

Brent shook his head again as he smiled wider. My pace reduced to almost walking speed.

"Well, you sure don't look it."

Lola whacked him on the shoulder with her magazine. "Lay off, will you? Give an old lady a break. I gotta get back to work." And with that Lola grabbed her cigarettes and lighter and went outside.

I notched up my speed but kept an eye on Brent in the mirror as he headed for the free weights. Whitney Blaire called him the ultimate hottie and said she'd do anything to be seen with him. When I asked why she didn't go after him, she laughed and said he wasn't her type. She was right, though: Brent was hot. Seventeen, but looked twenty, amazing shoulder-length brown hair, bright green eyes, a sexy smile, and a body that wasn't bulky but was so muscular there wasn't an inch of fat on him. I noticed that bit as I watched him from across the room.

After finishing the miles, I headed over to the mats. I was rounding off something like twenty push-ups (the real ones, not those sissy girly ones on the knees) when I looked up. About thirty feet away, Brent was watching me with a weight resting against his chest. He smiled that sexy smile as our eyes met. Setting the weight back on the rack, he sat up.

I got to my feet and casually headed toward the free weights.

"Terri, is it?" he asked when I got closer.

"Tara," I corrected and shook his hand, hard. He shook it again, testing my grip, and smiled more.

"Tara," he said. "You mind spotting me on some heavier weights?"

And like that we were a couple. There was a comfort level with him that I hadn't felt in a long time, hadn't let myself feel—not since Dad. But with Brent, it felt right, natural; I trusted him. When I wasn't with the girls, I was with Brent. We knew that training came first, but we got around that rule by doing it together. After a five-and-a-half-year absence from soccer, he got me to play goalie while he tried to bend a shot past me. Then three or four times a week he'd run with me early in the morning, five to eight miles depending on my schedule. There aren't many guys who would regularly run long distances just because they liked the company. And he wasn't intimidated that I was stronger than half the guys in school. In fact it turned him on.

Maybe that's why it seems at least possible that there was something between him and Sanchez. Sanchez has that broad muscular body that is often only seen in enhanced photographs. If Brent were interested in guys, Sanchez would be his type. But Brent has never given any indication of going for guys. Or cheating. Not that I have noticed, at least.

And no one at school has ever mentioned anything about Brent swinging both ways. Not now, not before. I feel like someone played a cruel joke on me, just to make the thoughts haunt me at night. Part of me argues that I should take Brent back because the incident really wasn't true. That said, knowing the rumor is false still doesn't change the images swimming in my head.

My attention returns when Brent spots me watching him through the glass. He raises his eyebrows and jerks up his chin as he smiles. I nod back and hurry to the pool. I try to focus, but Brent's smile stays with me as I swim 100 meters, 200 meters, 500 meters. But it's only at about 700 meters that the idea of Brent also smiling at Sanchez starts to fade.

 *Pinkie*

TONIGHT IS IT. I'M (KIND OF) GOING OUT WITH NASH. AT least I hope so. I hope he can still make it. I hope he doesn't suddenly get called in to work and feel like he has to cover someone's shift, because he's that kind of nice guy who would help out anyone who asked for it and because he's saving up and could really use an extra night's tips. I call him to see if he wants me to bring a tape recorder to the lecture just in case he does have to work so he can hear it later on and not miss out on Dr. Wang Hall's very important discussion on emerging democracy. But Nash doesn't answer and I don't leave the message because I suddenly worry that if I do, that might make him think that he doesn't have to attend the lecture at all and that's the last thing I want to happen!

I remind myself to breathe. Think calming thoughts. Or at least pretend to.

Whitney Blaire teases that she's going to gate-crash the lecture, which I really hope she doesn't since that would not make me look good in Nash's eyes. On the other hand, I do try to get the girls to come with me since it would just be weird to go on my own. Tara says she needs to work on getting sponsorship for the marathon. Whitney Blaire, as soon as I say I want her to come, says if she wanted to listen to an old man lecture, she'd stay at home more often. Even David says he has more important things to do, like sister-proof his life. He also tells me to chill out, which is silly because I'm totally and completely calm.

To prove it, I write a letter to Mama as soon as I get home. I tell her everything I know about Nash and then Google him to find out more (he never said he won the state spelling bee when he was twelve or that he lives close to Tara's house). I mention the wink to Mama and ask her opinion of whether it was a wink or a twitch because after twenty-three hours, I'm no longer convinced it was a wink. I say everything that comes to mind about him, everything else I want to know, and everything I like about him. I ask her if I should change my last name when we get married. I hope Mama likes him, which she probably will, considering that she never speaks badly of anyone.

When I'm done, I sign it and kiss the letter before putting it in the shoe box with the other letters to Mama. Then I head down for dinner. I haven't even started my homework, but there's no way I'm missing the lecture.

After we've said grace, I mention the lecture. I don't, however, specifically mention Nash.

Daddy rolls his eyes as he serves the lasagna. "How interesting. You know, Mousie, you can just say you're going off to a rock concert instead. It's fine by me."

"Dino," Barbara scolds Daddy. "You should be glad that you have such a good teenager. You won't believe what some of the women in the PTA are going through with their teens. Besides, emerging democracy is a very important and controversial subject. Pinkie, have fun and take some good notes, but remember that you have school tomorrow so you shouldn't be out too late."

I nod and keep eating. Even after eleven years, eight months, two weeks, and four days, Barbara is still determined to be the "good" stepmom. Her latest bedside read, something like *Children Are from the Sun and Teenagers Are from Pluto*, must have told her to be supportive of a teenager's needs without being pushy. For the most part I get along fine with Barbara, but I can't tell her the things I tell the girls or Mama. Maybe because Barbara is so old. Not as old as Whitney Blaire's parents but still getting on. She's two years older than Daddy, which means she's too old for him. Not that Daddy is old, just normal mid-forties, but Barbara acts it while Daddy doesn't.

"Well," says Daddy after Barbara finishes her lecture on teenage philosophy and psychology, "if you really do end up going to a rock concert, and get completely wasted—"

"Are you encouraging our daughter to go behind our backs?" Barbara crosses her arms and pulls her shoulders back, which suddenly makes her look three times the size of a normal person.

Daddy, however, doesn't get intimidated. "No, I'm just saying, hypothetically, if it were to happen, you can always call and we'll pick you up no matter what."

Barbara relaxes a bit, which means her size returns to just over six feet tall, and turns to me. "Well, yes, Pinkie, your safety is the most important thing, but better to not get yourself in a pickle where you feel you need rescuing."

I scoop up some peas and carrots. "It's okay. I really am going to a lecture on emerging democracy."

"Good," says Barbara, and with that they don't ask any more questions.

My half sister Angela is another thing. Straight after dinner, she shows up while I'm brushing my teeth and asks who else is going.

"I don't know," I mumble.

"But will Nash be there?"

"He's the one who told us about it."

"Can I come?" Angela asks.

I spit out the toothpaste and look at her through the mirror. Ever since I had to babysit on a bowling evening and Nash insisted that I bring Angela along, she's been desperate to join us again. "It's a grown-up lecture with lots of old people. You won't understand anything."

Angela places her hands on her hips. "My teacher says I have the comprehension level of a fifteen-year-old."

I don't say anything. No one has ever told me I have a high comprehension level. Not in fifth grade, not ever. Does that mean that I don't? Is this going to reflect on my college applications next year? Are universities going to think that I'm not advanced for my age? What about these AP classes I'm taking? They have to count for something, right?

I take a deep breath. "Angela, this is a school trip. It's only for people who are in the club."

"I'm sure Nash won't mind and I really want to go."

"Why?"

Angela blushes. "Well, Nash . . ."

Now it's my turn to blush. Is Angela saying she has a crush

on Nash? And worse yet, am I jealous of my baby sister? "Nash is too old for you."

"He's only ten years older than me, which in a few years will be nothing. Just like your mom and Daddy."

I drop the spool of dental floss. How does Angela know my mama's age? I've never taken her to meet Mama. "Nash is eleven years older than you."

"Ten. I'm eleven next month."

I shake away the thought and head to my room for my things. Angela has always been prettier than me, with blue eyes and skinny legs. Even the brown hair we both have looks better on her than me. I don't like thinking that in a few years she'll be competition.

My phone buzzes to let me know it's time to head out. Angela tries one last time to convince me to let her come. She promises never to ask me for anything else again and tells me I'm the best sister in the whole wide world. Barbara finally butts in to say that Angela has to wind down and start getting ready for bed. I get a look of death from Angela since it's obviously my fault that Barbara won't let her go. I send my own look of thanks to Barbara.

I get to the lecture eight minutes early and search the room. I was right. There's no one under the age of fifty, let alone anyone from school. And no Nash. Maybe he's here and I can't see him? Is that him with the hat? No, that's a bald seventy-year-old man. What about that guy over there talking to a group of people? No, that's a woman. I double-check he's not in the room and then go back outside. I pull out my phone. It's turned on, I have it set to silent vibrate, and no, there are no missed calls or texts. Maybe he's in the bathroom. Should I poke my head in (with my eyes closed, of course) and call his name to see if he's there? But then they start flashing the lights to enter the room. I sit in the back and survey the crowd again. Still no one I recognize. Someone sits down next to me. I'm about to say the seat is taken when I realize it's him.

"Hey, I thought I'd be the only one," I whisper.

"Nah," he whispers back and hugs me, leaving an arm around my shoulder. "I wouldn't miss it."

The lecture starts. I realize I forgot to bring something to take notes. Then again, I don't even know if Dr. Wang Hall is speaking English. My mind is on Nash. He must have forgotten that his arm is around me. Or maybe it's just a casual thing. I glance his way. His eyes stay on the speaker, but his arm gives me a squeeze. Was that a general "glad you're here" squeeze or a "you're a good squeeze" squeeze? I don't move in case he suddenly realizes it was an "it was a mistake" squeeze.

Halfway through, Nash takes hold of my hand, although his other arm stays around me. I look at him again. He looks at me too this time and winks. Tentatively I clasp his hand a bit tighter. He responds by rubbing his thumb across the back of my hand.

Dr. Wang Hall finishes his speech with a small bow. Nash lets go of me for the first time and bursts onto his feet. A few other people stand up. I join them even though I hadn't heard a single word.

"The man is a genius," Nash says.

I nod and hope that's good enough.

"Shall we go?"

"Yes," I say quickly.

He holds my hand again, as we walk slowly out to the cars.

The days are getting colder, but I feel extremely warm with him next to me. We stop in front of his little two-door.

"I'm glad no one else from school came," he says. "It was really nice having you to myself."

He looks at me with that look that says any minute now he's going to lean forward.

My mind goes light speed. Did I brush my teeth? I think so, but what if it's not fresh anymore? What if I'm not a good kisser? Am I even allowed to kiss a teacher? But he's not a teacher. He's Nash.

His lips touch mine and my mind goes blank. I think I wrap my arms around him; I think at one point I put my hand on his face to see if it's smooth, but if it is, I don't remember. It's all so tingly and nice, I don't know what's going on. I just go along with it.

Too soon, he moves his lips away but his arms stay around me. "Sorry, it's getting late. But can we do something over the weekend?"

"Definitely." I don't have to give it any thought.

"Awesome." He kisses my nose and lets go. "I'll call you."

"Great!"

"Bye."

"Bye," I say, and watch him drive away. My feet are rooted to the ground, but my head seems to have detached itself to float in the clouds. For a second I imagine what it would be like to call home and say I need rescuing. I'm sure I can't remember the way back. Instead, I stay in the parking lot for twenty-three minutes—that's how long it takes to get myself calm enough to drive home. Hopefully I won't get lost.

Whitney Blaire

I'VE FINISHED MY SALAD AND AM NOW HELPING MYSELF to the last of David's fries. It's the ultimate skinny rule: as long as you don't order the food yourself, the calories don't count. Besides, the iceberg and fries cancel each other out like positive and negative numbers so it's like I'm practically eating nothing.

"So then . . ." I pause for effect but David isn't paying attention to me. Instead, he has this little goofy smile on his face and is half blushing. He smiles like that at me sometimes, and it's really cute, but it's not me he's smiling at now. I turn my head around to see what's making him gawk.

There's a girl I've never seen ordering food. And it's not just David; every guy in the place has gone gaga checking her out. Don't ask me why. For one thing she's ugly as all hell. Her black hair looks like some kind of moth-eaten Halloween wig. As for her clothes, all I can say is that there's a difference between being a size 1 and squeezing into it. And the worst is that she's just a kid. She's some little kid that went crazy with her mother's makeup and stole an older sister's bra to stuff with tube socks.

"Damn," David whispers.

"Who's that?" I demand.

David shrugs, his eyes still on the kid. "A tourist?"

"No tourists would come to this town."

"Maybe she's visiting someone. She can come visit me anytime."

I hit him on the back of the head.

"What?" He turns away from the kid and stares at me.

"David, she's like ten years old. That's gross. Besides, you shouldn't stare." I shove down two more fries. I don't care if me and David are never going to date in a million years. It's totally wrong for him to act like a guppy.

David returns to what's left of his fries. "I just wanted to see what everyone else was looking at. Besides, no way that girl's ten."

I look at her again. I know that if I was standing, she wouldn't be much higher than my shoulders. And that's without my heels. With heels, she wouldn't reach my chest. No, David's right. She's not ten. More like eight.

The girl walks by us with her takeout bag. By the smug look on her face, I can tell she thinks she's the shit and loves the fact that everyone is staring at her. She flicks her hair and swishes her hips. It's like she's daring someone to try and steal her attention. When she passes by us, she turns up her nose.

I turn my head around to look at her over my other shoulder. In the second it takes to change directions, a big figure blocks the light coming in from the door.

I recognize Brent, the Abercrombie lookalike, right away. Of course everyone else looks at him too. According to Tara, they're taking a break, which I kind of feel like it's my fault since I told her about that stupid thing, but maybe she has others reasons. But until she says she's done with him for good, he's not up for grabs. Of course the eight-year-old doesn't let that stop her.

"Excuse me." She places a hand on his arm. It looks like she's moving him out of her way. It also looks like a sneaky way to feel up his arm.

Brent steps slightly to the side and gives her the once-over. "Hi. You need help carrying that?" He gestures to her takeout bag as if it were heavy.

"No, that's okay." The girl smiles up at him.

"You look really familiar." He runs a hand through his hair. "Do I know you from school? Or maybe I've seen you on TV?"

She laughs and sticks out a hip. Her belly ring flashes as it catches the sun. "Not on something you'd want to watch," she says.

Still, he raises his eyebrows and winks. "I wouldn't be so sure."

I push down the stupid plastic salad lid. It doesn't close. I keep trying, but it just makes a lot of noise. Not enough noise, though. Brent carries on, "So, what's your name?"

"Riley."

Brent smiles. "I like that. Riley. I'm Brent, by the way."

I have to do something. She's all over Brent and I'm not going to let some little kid steal my best friend's boyfriend.

"Brent, hi!" I call out. Leaping from my chair, I rush to hug him. I link my arm through his and hope he doesn't pull away. "I didn't know you were here."

I glimpse the little girl trying to duck out. And then, I honestly don't know what happened next. Seriously, I just stretched out my leg when all of the sudden, the girl is sprawled out on the floor. Her bag breaks and then there's baked potato and orange juice all over the place. (Who goes to a burger joint for a baked potato and orange juice anyway?)

I look down at her as if I'm noticing her for the first time. "Oh, what happened? Are you okay?"

"Fine," she snaps. What a bitch.

"Oh, man." Brent holds out a hand. "Here, let me help."

"I said I'm fine." She looks from me to Brent and gets up on her own.

"Brent, be a dear and get us some napkins." I smile sweetly at him. The second he leaves, I glare back at the girl. "He's taken, so don't even think of stealing him away. Or I will hurt you."

The look the girl gives me is cold, but I don't shiver. "You? Hurt me? With those fake nails?"

I'm about to say the ultimate comeback: something cool, something smart. Something any second now. But David gets between us and starts dragging me away. "Whitney, we got to go, because that sale my sister was telling us about at the mall, it's going to end in like five minutes."

I try to break away, but David leads me out of the burger joint. I turn around and see that Riley kid come out the door, alone. Good. Maybe she got the hint.

A few blocks down, and out of sight of the burger joint, I finally shake off David's hand.

"A sale at the mall? How superficial can you make me look?" I place my hands on my hips. Okay, so yes, I do shop at any store that has a sale, but did he have to go and broadcast it to the whole world?

"C'mon, I had to get you out of there. That girl would've clobbered you."

"She's a shrimp."

"She's a fit shrimp. Did you see her shoulders and that six-pack?"

Her ugly belly piercing, not to mention the fact that she was practically jumping Brent's bones, kept me from looking at her body. But it doesn't help my mood that David had noticed it.

David is still going. "I mean, that girl was something. Like a small, dark Tara, but with curves—"

"Shut up."

"—no wonder he was after her," David finishes.

"I said shut up!" I hiss under my breath. "Such a bitch."

David doesn't say anything for a while. He keeps his hands shoved in his pockets as he kicks a pebble down the sidewalk. We walk a bit more before David finally says something. "Do you want to go home?"

"No," I answer quickly.

Silence again.

David makes a sound in his throat. "You know, I think Sophie did mention something about a seventy-five-percent-off summer clearance."

I lick my lips and turn to look at him. "Which store was this?"

When I get home with my bags, the entire house is spotless as usual. Mother has Carmen come about twice a week to clean, whether the house needs it or not. It never does; nobody's ever home to dirty it. Sometimes I want to spit on the counter, just to make a mess. But then Carmen would make me clean it up.

And cleaning is one thing you can't pay me to do. Besides, it's hard to tell when someone will be home. There's no point in making a mess to make a statement if no one's around to notice the statement, or the mess. My parents usually aren't home, but sometimes I get surprised.

I'm not surprised today, though. My voice echoes through the house when I call out. When they're in, Father reminds me not to shout and Mother goes on about the effectiveness of a calm tone and how I should use the intercom instead. I don't have to look on the kitchen counter to know that Mother has left a twenty. She used to leave a note as well, saying that she and Father were working late and that I should order a pizza. In those notes she would even mention what time they'd be back and where I could reach them in case of an emergency. Nowadays, especially if they're just working late, she doesn't usually bother with a note. She just leaves the cash.

I grab the money and make my way through the house. I pass the lounge and Father's study as I head up the stairs. I know without trying the door that it is locked. Father's study is only ever unlocked when he's actually in it, but even then I have to knock before entering. At the top of the stairs to the right is my parents' room. That room isn't locked, but I don't usually bother going in there.

On the wall between Mother's study and one of the guest bedrooms are the family photos. Not the kind at Pink's house taken yearly at Sears with everyone looking happy because they're all wearing matching snowman sweaters. The photos on our wall show our successes: Father after he won a multimillion-dollar case; Mother receiving the Citizens' Choice award for the area's favorite therapist; both of them with the vice president. The one of me was taken when I was three and crowned Little Miss Tiny Tot.

Farther along is another guest bedroom, a bathroom, my former playroom—which has been converted to my study, though I never use it for that—and then finally my bedroom with its own bathroom. My room has always been the farthest away from my parents'. Which means it's the best room in the house.

I dump the bags on the floor and put the twenty in the leather wallet I keep between my sweaters on the top shelf of my closet. I can barely reach it so I know Carmen definitely can't, though I don't think she would. No one else comes into my room, so I know it's safe. Then I call Pink to see if I can come over for dinner.

 *Pinkie*

NASH HASN'T CALLED. I WONDER WHETHER HE LOST my number. I wonder if he ever had it. The whole group exchanged numbers at the beginning of the year, but he might not remember the list. I've called him a couple times before when I've needed his help with some trig problems. Always left a message. But he's never called back. Probably because he was at work and figured I had solved the problem by the time he got the message. Which I had, but it still would have been nice if he had called back. But then again, how could he if he didn't have my number?

I give him until four o'clock on Saturday and then call him up.

"Hi Nash, this is Pinkie, Pinkie D. Ricci. I thought we were doing something this weekend and since I haven't heard from you, I was just making sure everything is all right. Can you give me a call? Maybe we can do something tonight or tomorrow, that is if you're free and if you're interested. So yeah, let me know if you're all right and I hope to see you soon. Here's my number."

I hang up and instantly think I've given him the wrong number. Should I call him again and make sure? No, that probably falls under the category of stalker. But on the other hand, what if I really did give him the wrong number? What if he's trying to call back now and can't get me? The missed-calls menu on his phone could be broken.

I pick up the phone and press the button that calls back the last number. "Nash, hi. It's Pinkie D. Ricci again and I'm sorry, I don't know if I gave you the right number. It's . . ." I say it slowly to make sure I don't mess it up. And then for good measure, I leave it one more time.

 *Tara*

WHENEVER I SEE BRENT IN THE HALLWAYS, HE SMILES
and raises his eyebrows. Sometimes I smile back. But I make
sure he keeps his distance. I don't want him to touch me. I can't
let him. Sometimes we chat, usually about sports and training.
We don't mention what he says didn't happen last week.

I need to focus on my training. The marathon is only eight
weeks away. With my inconsistent times, I need to get back in
form. Just because there are rocks on the trail, I can't let them
trip me up.

I am only doing four miles today. Marathon training is
varied. There are days for short sprints and there are days for
going the distance. Sometimes the race course involves going
up and down hills. Sometimes the weather on the race day isn't
ideal. These are the things I need to work on: running under
any condition.

Four miles go by before I realize it. When I read the
numbers on the stopwatch, I grin. That's the way to do it.

Seven seconds better than last week's four miles at a moderate speed. Welcome back.

Mom drops me off at school on her way to work. Pinkie's been giving me rides again this last week or so, but her car's in the shop and the alternative is going in Barbara's minivan along with five ten-year-olds. I know Whitney Blaire is getting a taxi; she'd rather spend the money than go in the minivan, or worse yet, get her parents to drop her off.

I wave to my mom and head for the doors. Brent is chatting with his teammates on the wall. He jumps down when I pass by. Before I can duck, he kisses me on the cheek.

"Brent," I warn, but he doesn't pay attention.

"Hey, we're rounding up the guys for some ultimate during lunch. You want in?"

I do. I'm always up for an impromptu game. But playing Frisbee with Brent brings back too many memories of other times we've played: our awareness of the other's presence, our ability to predict the other's next move, the natural teamwork connection that's stronger than what Brent has with his soccer team. And then there were the little special moments of hidden smiles and secret gropes that the others didn't see. I don't trust him to keep his hands to himself. I'm not sure if I trust myself either.

"I'm meeting the girls for lunch."

Brent frowns just as the bell rings. "Too bad. Maybe next time." He picks up his bag and slaps me on the butt before walking off.

I take a deep breath and let out the air slowly. I join the crowd as I head to Spanish class. I've been watching him since that day Whitney Blaire told me the rumor. Watching how he acts with the girls, and the guys. I don't notice anything more than his normal friendliness. I've even seen him chatting with Sanchez and there's nothing to imply an attraction. Not from Brent, at least. Sanchez, on the other hand, makes it very obvious that he wants something. But that's how Sanchez acts with everyone. It bothers a lot of the guys (and me too), but Brent just ignores that bit and treats him like he treats everyone else. At least, he doesn't encourage Sanchez. I want to think that just means Brent is confident in himself—that he's simply not threatened by a gay man—but I'm still not entirely sure. And until I am, I have to keep things neutral with Brent. Be strong, Tara, I tell myself. Just give yourself some time.

I settle down in my seat in the middle of the classroom. Pinkie is already sitting in the front with her reading glasses on. She gives me a half wave and then gets back to the textbook in front of her. We're having a quiz today and Pinkie always studies until the last second. I don't have to look to know Whitney Blaire isn't here yet. Even when Pinkie drives her in the morning, Whitney Blaire is never on time for anything.

Ms. Ramirez starts closing the door and Whitney Blaire sneaks in just in time. She walks by my desk and drops a note. It says: *iv som thn 2 tel u* with a heart on top of the *i*. I crumple the note and stuff it in my pocket before Ms. Ramirez sees it.

Ms. Ramirez hands out the quizzes right away and I forget about Whitney Blaire's note. She doesn't, though. As I finish the first page, I get another note: *thrs a nw grl. boyz al ovr hr.* I crumple that note too and move on to the next page.

Ms. Ramirez passes by me. She grabs another note Whitney Blaire has just written.

"Señorita Blaire, see me after class," Ms. Ramirez tells her. Pinkie sends Whitney Blaire a scolding look.

"Class, I want your eyes to stay on your own papers. That includes everyone," Ms. Ramirez reminds us. Pinkie blushes.

Once the bell rings, I leave quickly for my next class, knowing that I'll get the full scoop at lunch.

And I'm right. According to Whitney Blaire, this eight-year-old munchkin cast a spell that made every sensible guy gawk at her. In other words, David took his eyes off Whitney Blaire for a couple minutes to look at someone else.

I half listen as I look out the window to catch part of the Frisbee game. I watch Brent leap into the air, grab the disc two others were trying to get, and send it sailing to another teammate in a matter of seconds. It looks like a great game. I sigh and turn back to the girls.

"Oh great, she's here," Whitney Blaire groans. "No, no. Don't look."

Of course I turn around right away. Pinkie's more discreet, holding up her compact mirror to sneak a peek.

"Where?" I don't notice an eight-year-old, and certainly no one resembling a munchkin.

"There. The one that looks like a witch."

I look again and this time I do spot a short girl. She probably isn't much more than five feet, but she's still normal looking and not any younger than the rest of us. But I don't give her shortness, or even her face, much thought. It's her hair that I notice: waist length, thick, shiny, and black. I've never seen hair that long look so healthy. My own blonde bob is limp from too many washings. It gets horrendously thin if I even let it grow close to shoulder length. But this girl's hair . . . I want to touch it. Make sure it's real. I want to know if it feels as nice as it looks.

As she gets nearer, Whitney Blaire hisses something like "bra stuffer," as if she should talk with her add-a-size padded push-up. The girl glances at me quickly as she passes. My hazel eyes meet her brown ones. I can't breathe. I can't move. It really *is* like she cast a spell. A lilac scent lingers as the black hair floats away.

"Who is she?" I finally manage to speak without gasping.

Whitney Blaire makes a gagging noise. "I told you. A total bitch."

But that can't be true, not of *her*.

 *Pinkie*

STILL NO WORD FROM NASH. I LEFT A THIRD MESSAGE ON his phone. And just to make sure that he's not deliberately avoiding me, I blocked my number and called him from home. He didn't answer and I didn't leave a message that time. I'm certain his phone isn't working. Whitney Blaire once had the problem that her phone deleted all her messages and wiped out half of her address book too. The same could have happened to Nash's phone. I know it isn't my phone. I already went down to T-Mobile to complain that I'm not getting calls and the guy there assured me that the phone is in perfect order. Part of me thinks that I should call Nash to let him know that his phone isn't working. I don't, of course, but only because calling one more time might make me seem a bit obsessed. Which I'm not.

Still, I run it by the girls at lunch.

"So, tell me, why don't boys return calls? Because it's not just Nash, is it? I mean, I've heard other girls complain about it, right? Please tell me it's not just me."

"Come on, Pink, of course it's you," Whitney Blaire teases. At least I hope she's teasing.

"It's not you." Tara sends Whitney Blaire a dirty look as she confirms. "Some guys are just like that. They forget."

"But everyone does that—girls too. I've gotten guys' numbers and then forgotten to call them," Whitney Blaire says as she drinks some of my chocolate milk.

"Forgotten to call, or forgotten who they are?" Tara teases.

"I know. I can be such a bitch sometimes." Whitney Blaire laughs, but I can tell she's proud of herself. "I should start taking pictures when I get a number. Then I'll remember the next day which one is worth calling."

They are getting off track. I turn to Tara. "How often did Brent call you?"

Tara shrugs. "I don't know. Every day or so."

My eyes widen. "But it's been five days since the lecture and still Nash hasn't called me."

"Well, he's a freak," Whitney Blaire puts in.

"Nash is not a freak! Do you think he's a freak?" I look at Tara, who is glancing at another table.

It takes her a second to reply. "Course not."

I look at the table that Tara was looking at. The girl that Whitney Blaire gossiped about is sitting with some of the school's weirdos. Maybe that's why Tara is staring at her, which is a bit unfair really. The new girl probably doesn't know those kids are weird.

I take a bite of the meat loaf and mashed potatoes. "So what do you think is up with Nash?"

"He's older. He could just be playing you," Tara says. This

time I catch her looking over at Brent. I want to do something to keep her from thinking about him, but I don't know what. I've always felt he wasn't right for Tara—too certain of his so-called charm—and am secretly glad she's taking some time away from him. I'll just have to keep talking and hope my problems need more immediate attention than hers.

"I don't think so," I say. "Nash always seems so happy to see me. I was starting to think he liked me as much as I like him, but maybe not. I wish there's some way to find out what's going on."

"Maybe there is." Whitney Blaire grins.

Tara takes her eyes off Brent and gives Whitney Blaire her full attention. "Don't even. I don't know what you're thinking, but it's not going to work."

Whitney Blaire takes another sip of my chocolate milk. "But if it does, Pink will love us forever."

"What?" I say. "What are you talking about?"

"Operation Spy on Nash."

I stop eating. The fork stays between my mouth and the plate. "What do you mean?"

"Don't do it," says Tara as she bites into her apple.

"No, really, it's perfect." Whitney Blaire keeps drinking more of my chocolate milk. "We get you all dressed up in some kind of disguise, Pink, and then go down to Lay Bone From-age—"

"*Le Bon Fromage*," I correct her.

She rolls her eyes and continues. "And then you can, what's the word, interrogate him. Flirt a bit, see what he's like when you're not around."

I squint at her. "How are you going to disguise me?"

Even though Tara was originally against the idea, she now suggests, "You can go in drag."

"No, that's just wrong." I know she's teasing, but I take things like that seriously. And she knows it. Which is probably why she said it to begin with. "And even if it weren't, do you really think I can boob-bind these two monsters?" I point down.

Tara turns away, but I still see her blush. "Sorry, I wasn't thinking."

"Nah, we need to keep you a girl so you can get close to him," Whitney Blaire says, and I can almost see her brain scheming away.

Even though part of me wants to know what Whitney Blaire is planning, it's time to be realistic. "But what if he recognizes me? I'll never be able to face him again. I'll have to transfer to another school. Change my name and—"

"Don't worry. You'll look so different, he won't even think about it. First off, does Barbara still have her whale outfit?"

I take a couple quick breaths. I don't like where this is going, but I answer anyway. "You mean that maternity dress we used to use as a tent?"

"Exactly. We stuff you with pillows and make you look fatter—"

"Fatter?" I reach for what's left of the chocolate milk. The straw makes the empty sound, but I still slurp a couple drops. "I know I'm rounder than you two sticks, but I'm not fat. Do you really think I'm fat?" I look from one to the other with the straw still in my mouth.

"Course not, I didn't mean it like that, I just—" Whitney Blaire starts, and then Tara cuts her off.

"You've got these great curves and you really are a healthy weight for your body type, Pinkie."

Slowly, I set down the chocolate milk. "Really?"

"Trust me." She puts the remains of the apple core on a napkin. "Fitness and nutrition are two of the few subjects I know more about than you do."

Tara does have a point, and seeing as that was settled, Whitney Blaire continues with her plot. "Then we dye your boring brown hair something wild, like purple or green, straighten it, and put load of makeup on. Really, when I'm done with you, your own mother won't recognize you."

My eyes widen. I've never thought about that. Mama, not recognize me? Is that really what it'll be like when I see her again? Me jumping up and down, waving, and passing right by? No, I can't let that happen.

I look at Tara for some help, but she's staring at the new girl again.

"Whitney Blaire," I begin, trying to think of a tactful way to refuse her help. "I don't think, I mean, I don't know if they'll let me into Le Bon Fromage looking like that."

"You're probably right." She takes a breaded mushroom from my plate. "Don't worry, I'll think of something else. One way or another, we'll figure out what's behind that boy of yours."

"I think you should just drop the games," Tara says. "And ask him straight up what's going on. If you think you can trust him."

Of course I trust Nash, but I could never ask him straight up. Then again, I'm not too thrilled about Whitney Blaire's spying idea either. I'll just have to wait and see. I finish the last of the potatoes and glance around the cafeteria.

The new girl is looking at us now. Tara doesn't notice but Whitney Blaire does. The two stare at each other. I watch Whitney Blaire mouth "f off" and the girl mouths back "up yours." Whitney Blaire crumples her chip bag and I know she's imagining it's the girl's head. Maybe I won't have to worry about embarrassing myself during Operation Spy on Nash now. I'd be surprised if Whitney Blaire even remembers the idea. She's found someone to hate and that will keep her busy for a while.

Whitney Blaire

WHO DOES THAT SKANKY NEW KID THINK SHE IS? I SAW the looks she was giving Tara at lunch. Then she'd go stare at Brent. I think Tara noticed it. I caught her looking at the kid too, but I don't think Tara knows the girl has her sights on Brent. I haven't told Tara, but maybe I should. The girl doesn't know who she's messing with if she thinks she has a chance with him, not while he's still kind of Tara's. But I can tell she's not going to back off easily. She didn't listen when I silently told her to mind her own business. I'm going to keep an eye on her. I don't trust her.

Especially since I saw her talking to Chris Sanchez. I used to get along fine with Chris. He always said the craziest things. Very graphic and blunt. Made me laugh. He's also the cheerleader with the best body. But he's dealing with the enemy now. I know Andre jumped the gun with the whole Brent-and-Chris thing, but I also know Chris would do Brent given the chance. He'd do it, brag about it, and think nothing of it that Brent was seeing Tara. And if I'm right about Riley, which I know I am, she'd do the same thing and that makes her just as bad.

Tara

I STOP BY THE GYM AFTER SCHOOL FOR LIGHT TRAINING on the free weights. I take the long way to the RTC and pass by the gymnastics area. Although anyone who pays the entrance fee can use the whole gym, the gymnastics area is restricted to those with special permission. I could probably get in if I wanted to, but there's no point. I could never do what they do. Maybe that's why I like watching them.

One class is tumbling on the mats. Some little girls are walking on the ground balance beams. A few older girls are standing around talking to their coach. I wait a couple of minutes. One girl breaks away from the group, rotating her shoulders. She chalks up her hands and then brushes off the excess on her thighs. I rest my forehead against the glass. She does this little skip hop before sprinting down the runway. A round-off onto the springboard leaves her back to the vault. Still, her hands land on the vault and suddenly she's twisting and turning in the air. No sooner does that happen then she's back on her feet, taking a step to the side to regain her balance.

The coach starts waving his hands and the girl nods as she walks back to where she started. She chalks up again. Once more she sprints and does her round-off. There's more power this time as she lands on the springboard, and after pushing off from the vault, she has more height as she flips in the air. When she comes down, she lands square on her feet. I clap. She looks pleased as she wipes her hands on her legs again. Her teammates and coach are nodding and clapping too. Then she looks through the large window and sees me watching from the gym above.

I get away from the glass as quickly as I can and dart to the changing rooms. When I get there, my heart is beating as if I've already worked out.

Shit.

With her hair all pinned up, I had no idea it was her. There's nothing wrong with watching the gymnasts—that's why the window is there. But that doesn't change the fact that I've now been caught twice staring at the same girl.

Breathe. In and out. Drink some water. Focus on the weights, training, reps, sets.

I go through my strength training and then my shower without thinking about anything other than the exercise. That's the only way to do it. I have to stay focused. In control.

I'm fully dressed and toweling my hair when the changing-room door slams. I freeze. It's not the door; it always slams. It's the fact that the girls are covered in pasty chalk and talking about how hard the damn vault is.

I lower my head. I will not look at her again. I rummage through my bag and wonder if I can get out unseen.

"Sorry," says a voice. I want to hide. Without looking up, I know it's her. "Can I get to the locker next to you?"

"Uh, sure," I mumble as I shift out of the way.

I can feel her body heat next to mine. I should explain, apologize. "Look, I—"

I give in and raise my eyes. Bits of hair are sticking up from the crown of her head. She has a sweet smile on her face. She doesn't seem mad that I've been staring at her. In fact, she looks nice. I relax and say something else that's on my mind.

"That vault you did was great."

She smiles wider. "Thanks. It's a killer. That's one of the few times I've gotten it right. My name is Riley." She holds out her hand. I shake it. It's sweaty and chalky, but I don't care. It's a good handshake, strong and confident.

"Hi. I'm Tara."

I finish putting everything in my bag, but I don't want to leave. I look in the pockets for something to do. I find Brent's old comb. I take my time running it through my wet hair. It's too short to tangle, but at least it seems like I'm doing something.

"So, did you just move here?" I ask.

Riley nods as she pulls pin after pin out of her hair. Already she has about fifty in her hand. "Almost two weeks ago."

"And how do you like it?"

Riley shrugs. "It's okay. I'm really lucky to train with this new coach. The gym is the biggest perk."

I grin. It's a good gym. I'm proud of it.

"I guess it'll get better once I start meeting some more people," Riley continues.

"I'll introduce you to my friends." I'm not usually sociable right off the bat, but I like Riley and I want her to like me. "We can meet by the front doors before the bell rings tomorrow."

Riley stops herself from making a face. "You're friends with that girl Whitney, right?"

I look at the comb. That's right. How did I forget that Whitney Blaire basically declared her the Wicked Witch of the West? I was so busy trying to forget the times she caught me staring that I missed the fact that Whitney Blaire made me look at her in the first place. But then again, I would have noticed a girl like Riley.

"Ah, I forgot you've met her."

"No, I haven't. I ran into her," Riley says. "Literally."

I don't know what to say. I wasn't there when Whitney Blaire and Riley first bumped into each other; I don't know what happened between them. But I know Whitney Blaire and she does go overboard sometimes.

"Maybe when you get to know her things will be different? She might be a bit of a drama queen, but when it comes down to it she's a real friend."

Riley shrugs. "Well, maybe I can give Whitney another chance."

"Whitney Blaire," I correct.

Riley raises an eyebrow. "Are there other Whitneys around?"

"No, she's the only one. But we've always called her by her full name. Everyone has. It's part of her image. Except for David, but that's just the way he is."

Riley doesn't say anything. Her hand is full of bobby pins and her hair is flowing over her body in soft waves. It looks even prettier up close than other times I've seen it. I actually have to ram my hands in my pockets because I want to touch it so bad.

"Look, I'll talk to Whitney Blaire beforehand and clear things up. And my other friend Pinkie is great, she gets along with everybody. Between those two, they can introduce you to loads of people. And if you're up for a lunchtime game, we can organize something with Brent—"

"You know what, I'm sorry. I forgot I'm busy tomorrow." Then Riley grabs her towel and heads for the showers.

I'm left there, with an old comb, wondering what I did wrong. She doesn't look back, but she left a trail of lilacs behind her.

 *Pinkie*

WITH NASH STILL NOT CALLING ME AND ALL MY FRIENDS doing their own activities, I'm feeling a bit lonely. Even Angela has plans today (which shows how desperate I am for company that I want to hang out with a ten-year-old). It's too early to start homework and there's nothing good on TV. The house is very quiet. Maybe a little too quiet. I don't like it. I don't feel safe in a quiet house by myself.

I grab Mama's letters from the shoe box and head out. Instantly I feel better. It's the empty house that always does it. Too many memories. Too many thoughts about what happened the last time it was this quiet. And the days haven't gotten too cold, so it's a shame to stay indoors.

I park on the road and walk through the gates. There are other people there, walking around and visiting family members or friends. I nod to them but don't speak. I sit down at Mama's side and start telling her everything that has happened. Some of the things I tell her are in the letters, but I know she would rather hear them directly from me.

I tell her about Nash and how much I think she would like him. I tell her how I know that I came on too strong. I wonder if my breath had been bad even though I had brushed my teeth. I also think he is embarrassed about what happened after the lecture. Then I tell her how I'm afraid that he might think I'm too young for him, even though I don't feel an age difference when we're together.

I tell her the stuff that I don't tell Barbara because she's too old to understand. Mama listens when I say what's going on with my friends and how it bothers me that Tara is not staying away from Brent and how Whitney Blaire is leading David on. I talk to her about school and about the colleges I'm starting to look at. She doesn't judge me when I admit to playing hooky the other week. I ask her if there is any way I can turn back time and at least change that day I missed to an excused absence. Just so it's not on my record.

I often ask her if there's a way to turn back time when I visit, even though it's stupid. I like to think of it as a game we play. An impossible game. Because if I could turn back time, then maybe Mama would still be here.

But she's not. I have to settle for placing her letters in a hole under the marigolds. Then I cover the letters with dirt for Mama to read.

 *Tara*

MOM GETS HOME JUST AS I'M TAKING THE CHICKEN OUT of the oven. I make room on the counter for the canvas grocery bags she brings in. It's a tight squeeze with the two of us and Sherman romping around with excitement. Mom gives me a quick hug and then heads upstairs to change out of her work clothes. Sherman trots after her and suddenly there's a lot more room in the kitchen.

I put away the groceries but leave out the yogurt for the fruit salad. I take the broccoli and carrots out of the steamer and divide them onto two plates. Mom returns later in a paint-covered T-shirt, cutoffs, bare feet, and no bra. Her long auburn hair falls in loose curls. I've always wished I looked more like Mom. Instead I've got Dad's thin, straight, dull hair. And his long face and strong thighs. And yet people ask if Mom and I are sisters. They're probably being polite, because unfortunately there's no resemblance.

She serves us both some brown rice and chicken. "Good day today?"

"It was all right," I answer. "School's the same. And I went to the gym for some weight training." I tell her about meeting Riley but leave out the part about me staring at her and my obsession with her hair. I don't know how Mom would react to that. I don't even know how *I'm* reacting to that. I just mention that Riley is a gymnast and new but doesn't seem interested in meeting my friends.

Mom cuts a piece of chicken. "It takes a while to get used to things when you're new. She's probably just a bit scared and shy."

I don't think Riley is shy. She introduced herself to me. She wasn't the one blushing when our eyes met. But then again, she hadn't been the one caught staring. I put that thought aside and ask Mom about her day. She sighs and goes on about the usual office complaints and how she feels she can never do anything right. I only half listen. It isn't that I don't care; I do and I hate seeing Mom so miserable, but it is pretty much the same thing every night. Mom keeps talking and my thoughts go back to Riley and her hair.

Once I finish dinner, I put down my plate for Sherman to clean and grab a couple bowls for yogurt and fruit salad. Mom is done complaining so I go back to my own subject. "I think I'd like to get to know Riley better. She seems really nice."

"She probably is and there's no reason why you shouldn't."

"What about Whitney Blaire?"

Mom places her own plate on the floor for Sherman. "You have other friends besides Whitney Blaire and Pinkie. There's no reason why Riley can't be one of them."

"I know that, but . . ." I scoop the fruit into the bowls.

Mom seems to understand what I can't say. "Whitney

Blaire might never like this girl, but see how it goes. Who knows, the four of you might really get along." Mom reaches over and squeezes my hand.

"I don't know," I say. Whitney Blaire is pretty stubborn. She's a great friend but a horrible enemy. Although there have been a couple times I've seen her change friends and enemies around. "Maybe you're right. I shouldn't let Whitney Blaire keep me from getting to know Riley. Thanks, Mom."

She shrugs and half smiles as if to say that's what moms are for. "Oh, I completely forgot. I picked up the mail."

"Is there—?" I start.

"Yes. Something you've been waiting for."

I don't even realize I'm holding my breath until Mom hands me a fat envelope and I let the air out.

I force a smile. "Great, it's the race information." I open it up and glance at the marathon booklet stating how the race day will work, ads for equipment, and tips on nutrition and avoiding an injury. It also includes lists of potential charities and how to best approach people for sponsorship. I was hoping the packet would come this week, but I can't say that I was waiting for it. Not like the letter I really want. It's been over a month since my seventeenth birthday in September, which means it's been over a year since I last heard from my dad.

Whitney Blaire

I CAN'T BELIEVE IT. TARA HAS MADE FRIENDS WITH THAT stupid Riley kid. It's horrible. It's like Pink and I are no longer good enough for Tara because we're not hard-core jocks. But really, what does Riley have that we don't? Nothing. Riley's not in the Honor Society like Pink and I'm much more fun to be with than her. Riley is just a nobody.

Just yesterday Tara said she couldn't hang out with Pink and me because she was going to the gym with Riley. What does she see in her? Pink and I, we're Tara's real friends. We have history. We were there when her father bailed years ago to Uruguay or Paraguay or something ending in "guay." We helped her out when she was in crutches for weeks because of a sprained ankle. And we spent hours looking for her that day a few weeks ago when I stupidly mentioned the thing with Brent and Chris. Riley wouldn't do any of that. I know she wants Brent for herself. She pretends she doesn't by avoiding him, but I see her watching him and Tara whenever they're talking. She stares and stares, watching their every move. If

Brent touches Tara's arm, I can see the smoke coming out of Riley's nose. But when Tara talks to Riley, she's all smiles. Damn hypocrite.

Then Pink has to go and invite her to eat lunch with us. I almost take my tray somewhere else, but Pink convinces me to stay. "Come on, Whitney Blaire, let's give her a chance. She's new and doesn't know many people. And Tara seems to think she's nice. Ooh, and look, they have nachos today. I'll go get us some."

I set my tray down. "With jalapeños."

Tara and Riley sit down a couple seconds later. I glare at her and she glares back. I know Tara had to convince her to sit with us too. But I got the better end of the deal. I don't see nachos on her tray.

Pink comes back with two tubs of nachos. "Sorry, they were out of jalapeños."

Figures. I take a chip and push it around the sauce. How am I supposed to eat them now? Without the jalapeños, the calories won't burn away.

"So," Pink, the damn welcome committee, says, "how are you finding it here? Do you like it?"

"It's all right," Riley answers.

"That's good," Pink says. She eats one the nachos. No one says anything. Pink offers Riley the tub. Riley takes the biggest one with the most cheese. Greedy pig.

I look at Tara. She's eating her usual healthy weird shit. And for some reason she's smiling. I eat a nacho and pretend I'm smiling.

"So," Pink starts again, "why did you move here?"

Riley unwraps her sandwich. "My parents didn't like who I was dating."

"Really? Parents really do that kind of stuff? Move to a whole new place just to keep you away from someone?" Pink asks.

Riley nods. "Mine did. Though they were offered better jobs over here anyway, so I guess that helped the decision."

"And did it work?" Tara looks at her.

Riley looks back at Tara. "We were going to break up anyway, so yes. But if that wasn't the case, nothing would keep me from seeing whoever I want."

I stare at her, just waiting for her to sneak a glance at Brent; she's practically saying she'll do anything to get him. But her eyes stay on Tara. Sneaky. There has to be another way I can get her. Then I remember what she didn't mention at the burger joint.

"Why don't you tell us about being on TV?" I suggest, thinking now she'll be embarrassed.

"You were on TV?" Pink gasps. I kick her under the table and she squeaks, which is worse than the gasp because it sounded like excitement. But at least it shut her up.

Riley looks surprised and then shrugs. "It's not that big a deal. I qualified for the national finals earlier this year and they showed me on the vault. I didn't win the event, but I guess the national news thought I was competition."

Liar, stupid liar. Okay, so maybe she was on TV for some silly air-flippy thing, but what about the other stuff? The secret thing she hadn't wanted to mention to Brent. Or had that just been a stupid act to create mystery and attract attention? That makes it worse.

But I can't think about it right now. The worse has gotten worse.

David is at the table.

"What are you doing here?" I demand.

He looks down at his shoes. "Just wanted to say hi."

Riley suddenly becomes all smiles and holds out her hand. "Hi, I'm Riley. I've seen you around, but I don't know your name."

David turns red and smiles like a dork. "It's all right. I've seen you too. How's it going?"

"Great," Riley answers as she slowly runs her hands through her hair, which of course is just an excuse to stick out her chest. "Ah, I'm really glad you came by. It's good to finally meet you."

My eyes squint to narrow slits and my nose flares. I wonder how easy it would be to hide the evidence if I were to scalp her. But no matter. Even if I'm caught, I have access to the best lawyer in town. And no one messes with my father.

"His name's David," Pink says, being her stupid overly friendly self. I kick her again but manage to hit the table instead. I scrunch up my face to keep from screaming. David blushes more and smiles bigger.

"Oh right, sorry. Yeah, it's David. Hi." He rocks back and forth on his feet. Any minute now he's going to wet himself.

I pick up the nacho tub and throw it at Riley.

"Lay off David and lay off Brent, you ho." And I storm out of the cafeteria.

That Riley is going down. And I'll make sure it gets done.

 *Pinkie*

I MATCH UP THE CORNERS PERFECTLY AS I FOLD THE napkins into triangles. It's been well over a week since the lecture and I haven't seen or heard anything from Nash. I've asked a couple of the other kids in the club, but they haven't heard when we're having our next meeting. I've driven by Le Bon Fromage a few times (okay, before and after school every day of last week). Sometimes his car is there and sometimes it isn't. Which means he's not working all the time, so he must have some free time to return calls. I'm so desperate to know what's going on that Whitney Blaire's spying idea is starting to sound good. But no, I won't. What I really need is someone who knows what guys think.

"Hey, Pink," David says.

"What?" I look up from the napkins. "Sorry, did you say something?"

"I asked till what time we have to be here today."

"Three. Two if we clean up fast," I answer quickly while

my mind stays on Nash and his broken dialing finger. I finish with the napkins and move on to restocking the tea basket.

Being youth leaders at our church means that David and I do anything anyone tells us to do before or after the service or at any charity event. Even though it's a Saturday, we agreed to help for a special service. Whitney Blaire calls it slave labor, but it gets us in free to any of the youth events. Besides, colleges like to see a lot of volunteering and active members of the community on the applications.

I look up, suddenly realizing the Nash answer might be right there in front of me.

"David, can I ask you a guy question?" I reach into the big box of teas and refill the basket with Earl Grey and Passion. The church always runs out of Passion the quickest.

"Sure, as long as it's something you can say in church."

I roll my eyes as I try not to blush. Jeez, where had he come up with that idea? But the more I try not to think about what David had said without actually saying it, the more heat I can feel rising on my face. Argh! It's the Passion herbal tea I drank earlier, I know it. "No, it's nothing like that, it's—"

I quickly grab the bag of cookies and organize them on a plate: chocolate, vanilla, chocolate, vanilla. This is so stupid. I'm almost seventeen years old and I still blush like I'm Angela's age whenever someone, especially a boy, makes any kind of joke like that. Besides, he's not a real boy, just David. I've known him forever. Our mamas used to throw us in the tub together. Great, Pinkie, you just have to go and remember that. Now you're blushing more than ever. I take a deep breath. It shouldn't be any different than talking to Tara and Whitney Blaire, except he would know what guys think.

"Okay, say there's this girl," I start, but I say it more to the cookies than David. "And she calls you a couple times. But you don't call her back. Why not?"

"You're asking why I wouldn't call a girl back?" He lifts up a glass to see if it's clean. "Oh, I get it. You want to know why some guy hasn't returned your call."

"No, not me," I correct quickly. "It's purely a hypothetical question, for a friend. Why don't guys call girls back?"

"I don't know. Is she pretty?"

"Normal, I guess."

"Maybe he lost the number."

"I leave it every time I call, and sometimes say it twice."

David looks at me with his eyebrows raised. "How many times have you called?"

"A couple times." I can feel David still staring at me. I fumble with the cookie bag. "Okay, I've called nine times, but I've only left three or four messages. And the last time I called him at work, but he didn't come to the phone even though I didn't say who I was."

David shakes his head. "Pink, you've got to give the boy a break. You're scaring him away."

I think about Nash, the smartest person I know, being scared of a girl calling him. "Would getting lots of calls from a girl scare you?"

"If it was Whitney, first I'd be psyched out of my mind, then I would think that someone was playing a sick joke. If it was anyone else, especially someone I didn't like, then yeah, I think I'd be a bit weirded out, thinking that she was obsessed and desperate."

I let that sink in. I know I come across as a bit obsessive

(but really it's just me being genuinely concerned), and when I don't hear back from people, I always imagine the worst. I don't want to be this genuinely concerned, but it's very easy to imagine people dead. Especially since people die all the time.

But desperate? I'm desperate to know why he's not calling, but I'm not desperate for him, am I? Is that what Nash thinks of me? Some desperate high schooler who thinks getting winked at and kissed in parking lots means something? Or maybe he thinks that I'll think he's desperate if he calls back quickly? Is that why it's taking him so long?

"Stupid." I rearrange the cookies when I realize there are more vanilla ones than chocolate. Now the pattern goes chocolate, vanilla, vanilla, chocolate. "I think if you like someone and want to talk to him, you should. Why wait for a later time when some unwritten law says it's okay to call? I mean, the other person should be flattered that you were thinking about him and that you didn't want to wait another moment to talk to him."

David finishes setting up the cups and leans against the table. "Who's this guy anyway? Maybe I've heard something or can ask around."

"Uh." I slip a broken cookie into my mouth. "I don't want to say."

"You're not like Whitney with this weird denial thing for Brent, are you?"

I almost choke on the cookie. "Eww, go—gosh no! Gross."

"All right then, just making sure. So who is it?" he insists as he helps himself to a cookie from the plate. I replace the one he took so that the pattern isn't broken.

"No really, I can't."

"It's Nash, isn't it?"

I don't answer and I know that tells David everything.

"But why?"

"Why what?"

"Why Nash? Is it because he's older?"

"No, of course not," I answer quickly. But then I realize that I'm not fooling either one of us. "Okay, maybe a little, but it's mostly because he's so amazing. He's really smart and knows so many things. He's funny, he gives great hugs." And his kisses are out of this world, but David doesn't need to know that.

David shakes his head like he doesn't believe me. Or doesn't want to. "You can do better. Nash is a phony."

"He is not!" I say, and then wonder whether he really could be a phony.

"He is. He gives us all this advice on how to get into universities and stuff, but look at him. He's in his twenties and has never been to college. I bet he never applied to Yale or Oxford, or wherever he claims he's going."

"Harvard. And of course he did! He's just saving his money. He works so hard, you should see him." Okay, I admit I've never seen him work, but that's because Le Bon Fromage is a really expensive restaurant and they don't let kids in without their parents. But he works hard for the Honor Society. It can't be easy setting up and organizing all that information for our biweekly meetings.

David tidies up the table, putting away the supplies we don't need and throwing away the trash. "If he works as hard as he says he does, he could make it work at Harvard. They have scholarships, you know. Hasn't he spent hours telling us about all sorts of grants, loans, and internships you can apply for? So why hasn't he done the same? I mean, he claims he's smart enough. I say he's chickenshit. Afraid that he won't get in and then what? Have to admit to everyone that he couldn't hack it."

I don't know what to say about David's comments. And I certainly don't want to think about it, which of course only *makes* me think about it. No, it can't be true. David is putting him down because he doesn't like him. But I don't know why David doesn't like him. Everyone likes Nash. Or at least they should. "Are you saying this to be mean?" I ask.

David looks like I've insulted him. "No, I just don't want you to get hurt."

Part of me wants to point out all the things that are wrong with his theory. After all, Nash has almost perfect SAT scores, the acceptances to the best schools, but the minimum wage he earns and the high cost of living make college a distant dream. But I've never actually seen the results, the letters, or his wages. I know what he has said and what Google has told me. I can only go by the fact that the school hired him as the advisor to the Honor Society, so surely they must have checked his credentials. "David, I don't want to fight with you."

"Fine. Who knows, I could be wrong."

"You are," I confirm. I'm tempted to call Nash and ask him if he's a phony. I don't believe David, not at all, but I want to hear it from Nash. But I won't call Nash, at least not today. I don't want to seem desperate. Because I'm not. Desperate.

Whitney Blaire

I FEEL LIKE SHIT. IT'S 11:15 ON A FREAKING SATURDAY morning. For what feels like the last hour, my darling mother has been nagging me through the intercom to come downstairs. Why doesn't she just let me sleep? What's her problem? I'm not at her beck and call. I have my own life, even if that just means sleeping. She doesn't control me.

I roll over but then I hear Father say my name through the intercom.

Swear, grumble, sigh. I get up and shuffle down to the kitchen.

Mother's fussing over something. She likes to pretend she does useful things around the house when really it's Carmen that takes care of everything. Mother has a hard time figuring out the dishwasher. I have no idea how she completed a PhD.

"Oh, darling, there you are. I've been calling you forever. I had to get your father to try. Didn't you hear me?"

I shake my head. "Were you outside my door?"

"Of course not, silly, I used the intercom. That's why we got it."

I shrug. "I didn't hear a thing. The system must be broken."

Mother sighs. "Again? They promised me it was the best but it's been nothing but faulty. I'm glad I paid for that five-year guarantee."

I don't say anything as I head to the espresso machine. I wonder if David or maybe even Pink can dismantle the intercom completely. They're supposed to be smart; it shouldn't be too hard for them.

Father walks in then. He glares at me over the old-man glasses perched on the end of his nose. I shift away from his espresso machine. I pretend I was reaching for hot chocolate instead. He's still staring at me.

"Good morning," I say.

"Morning," he replies. "How are your grades so far?"

"A's, top of the class."

"Good. That's what we like to hear." Then he picks up *The New York Times* from the breakfast table and returns to his study with it.

I go back to the espresso machine.

"Oh, darling, you don't have time for that."

I stare at my mother. "Why not?"

Mother makes faces at her reflection in the microwave. "We have appointments with Pierre in twenty minutes. My hair is an absolute mess and yours doesn't look much better."

She's not looking at me. She's not even looking at a dim version of me through the microwave. "And I set up appointments with Marissa for some waxing while we're there. Hopefully she can do something about those eyebrows you got from your father. They look like something you'd expect to see on some exotic animal."

"I plucked them last night," I tell her. She's given up on the microwave and is now rummaging around in her purse. She waves a hand in my general direction. I hate it when she does that.

"Of course you did, darling, and that's fine, but won't you feel better once Marissa works her magic touch?"

Again I keep quiet.

Mother waves a hand again, this time to dismiss me. "Hurry up and get dressed, we don't want to be late. And make sure you put on clean underwear. It's probably time for your bikini wax again. You don't have your period right now, do you?"

"Yeah, I do." Not really, but it's worth a shot if it gets me out of a bikini wax.

"Then make sure you use the super tampons. You don't want to bleed all over the place, now do you?"

I stare at her and wonder if it's worth telling her that Tara's mother thinks body hair is beautiful.

"Don't look at me like that, young lady. I was your age once. I used to get my period too, you know. Now hurry up, we're going to be late."

I come down ten minutes later and Mother takes another fifteen before we leave the house. We get to the salon a good forty minutes late for our appointments. Not that it matters. Pierre isn't ready for us. He never is, and yet he always charges for extra services. Mother never notices and I've never seen the point in telling her.

I go straight to the coffee machine at the salon. I add one sugar and one Sweet'N Low to my drink. I used to do two

Sweet'N Lows, but Pink claims that artificial sweeteners cause cancer in lab animals. Personally, I think that's bullshit (if it's true, then why are they legal?), but I humor her anyway.

I thumb through the magazines and drink the coffee while I wait my turn. Although I won't tell her, I'm glad Mother dragged me to the salon. My hair has been pissing me off for weeks. It's time for a change. And Pierre's a genius. He figured out that if he changed his name from Pete to Pierre, he can get paid more as a hairdresser by pretending to be ethnic. It adds to his exoticness and people pay for that. I can learn a lot about money from him.

And I guess I do need a bikini wax.

"Hi, sweetie." Pierre comes up to me and gives me a kiss on each cheek like they do in Europe. "I swear you must keep those boys begging for mercy. Come. Let's see if we can make you more gorgeous than you already are." Pierre leads me down to the chair.

I look over at Mother. She's sitting with foil on her head, explaining the basic psychology behind effective parenting to the woman next to her. She doesn't even remember I'm here. I wonder if she'd notice if I suddenly pulled out a gun and took Pierre hostage. Probably not. At least not for another half hour, until it was time for the next step in her hair treatment. So instead of pulling out a gun, I put on my public face and smile.

I reply to Pierre's teasing with a laugh. "Ah, but the one guy I want won't look at me." I wink at him.

He laughs. "Sweetie, when I'm done with you, even the gay boys will be on their knees, you're so gorgeous. So what will it be? Trim and touch-up on the highlights? Add a bit of body?"

I make a face while Pierre runs his fingers through my

hair. "I need something different. Maybe a little cut, but I think I'll go back to dark hair. Dark brown. And then with some burgundy highlights?"

Pierre closes his eyes for a second to imagine it. "Okay, I like it! You're right. Blonde is so yesterday and there are so many fake blondes it doesn't make a statement anymore. A rich dark brown is definitely the way to go, but not too dark or you'd go goth, and that wouldn't be a good look on you."

I nod. Dark hair is good. I also know that if Pierre really thinks it's a bad idea, he would suggest something else. And he's right about blondes, they aren't getting noticed anymore. It's people with dark hair who are turning heads these days.

It takes a few hours and a bit of pain (from Marissa waxing my legs and bikini line while the color sets) before Pierre lets me look in the mirror.

"Oh, sweetie, I love it," Pierre says as he blow-dries my hair. "I swear, if you were an actress, we'd start a craze all over Hollywood in two weeks tops."

I have to admit he's right. I look good. Damn good. I can't wait to show everyone.

Mother comes around then talking on her phone. She doesn't even look at me. She just gives Pierre a wad of hundred-dollar bills and blows him a kiss. Then she waves her hand for me to follow her to the car. Three guys' heads turn as I walk by. It's nice to have at least some people notice.

We drive off as Mother pushes multitasking to the extreme. At the moment, she's still talking on the phone, touching up her lipstick in the rearview mirror, and driving the car. With her so preoccupied, it's only moments before I can launch my plan.

She's talking to her secretary because she keeps going on about some patient and how she can't stop by the office on a Saturday.

"I have a family too, and we have prior commitments. I promised to spend the day with my daughter."

I didn't know that was the plan, and Mother probably didn't either, but I see my chance anyway.

"Shopping," I whisper.

Mother raises her penciled eyebrows. (She always has Marissa wax them off completely so she can match them with her mood of the day. Today, they are perfect arches. They make her look happier than she does on antidepressants.) "No I really can't, I need to get my daughter some school clothes."

I smile to myself. Perfect. Maybe I can get some shoes too, and then an early dinner at Lay Bone From-age. If I play it right, I might get to spy on Nash for Pink as well.

"Okay, fine," she says into the phone. "I'll see if I can swing by the office after we're done."

My smile disappears.

I pull out my own phone to play some music and notice a text from David. He asks if I want to see the new cheesy thriller with him this afternoon. I write that I just got my hair done and am now going shopping with my mother. He writes back immediately wondering what I look like. I tell him that I shaved most of it off and what's left is in rainbow dreads. He sends a laughing smiley and says to send him a picture and if I'm telling the truth, he'll pay me a hundred bucks. I would have told Mother to turn the car around to dash back to Pierre's but she's still on the phone. Instead, I check my makeup and realize I haven't put any on. I debate between staying as is or using my mother's. No question. Besides, I remember *Cosmo* saying that the natural look is back. Fluffing my hair a bit with my hands, I take six pictures and send him the best one. It takes him a few minutes to write back: DAM! WHEN CAN I COME OVER?!

I laugh and tell him in his dreams. But then I write that if he's still up for the movie, I'd text him when we're done shopping.

Pinkie

I SEE NASH FOR THE FIRST TIME SINCE THE LECTURE. IT'S been exactly two weeks (well, thirteen days and eighteen hours, give or take five minutes) since I last saw him. I've convinced myself that the moment we shared after the lecture was either imagined or a mistake, and that he's never going to have anything to do with me again. But now, he gives me his usual hug and he whispers, "I've missed you, *ma chérie.*"

He leads me to the space between the supply closet and the wall. He leans me against the wall with his hands on my hips. Then he kisses me and everything that I wanted to say to him melts away. The world is perfect: Nash is a god in human manifestation. Nothing else matters because I love my life. All my worries disappear. He does like me. This is real. And it's happening to me.

We break away as we hear someone approaching the door.

"This weekend," he whispers. "We'll definitely get together."

"When?" I have to know.

"I'm not sure. Maybe Saturday. I'll call you." He squeezes my hand as the door starts to open.

"Really, you'll call?" I ask as I straighten a desk.

Nash smiles as if I'm confirming that two plus two equals four. "Of course!"

During the rest of the meeting, Nash keeps winking at me or finding ways to brush my arm or back when he walks by. Nobody notices a thing except for David. He sends me looks of disapproval that I don't even get from Daddy. I just smile back. When the world is this perfect, I don't need to worry about the little things.

Whitney Blaire

THE GIRL IS PURE EVIL. SHE HAS A PLAN. IT INVOLVES TARA and Brent. It involves breaking up Tara and Brent for good. That's why she's getting friendly with Tara, to weasel her way in. Become an insider so that she knows all the secrets. Riley wants Brent for herself. But Tara doesn't listen when I tell her.

I see Riley up ahead. She's talking with some kid I don't know. I'm about to ignore her but then I hear Tara's name. And Brent's.

I slouch down against the lockers and I put on my sunglasses. I pull out a nail file and pretend I'm not there. With everyone walking around, Riley and the other kid don't even notice me. It's noisy, but I can still get what they say.

"So I hear Tara and Brent are getting back together," the kid says.

"It looks like it." Riley puts her hands behind her head. "They're meeting at the gym today at four thirty. It's the perfect setting for them to reunite."

The kid shrugs. "Maybe you can stop them? You'll be at the gym, won't you?"

"Yeah, but I'll be in training," Riley says. "I sometimes dream about what it'd be like to . . . No, I shouldn't think about that. But on the other hand, I can't stand it. I was starting to think I might have a chance."

The kid puts a hand on Riley's shoulder. "You never know. Brent might get bored with her."

Riley sighs. "I hope so. Brent doesn't deserve a girl like Tara."

I watch them walk away and then kick myself for not taking Riley out then and there. I knew she was up to no good and now I have the proof. Riley is after Brent. I just have to get to the gym this afternoon. And find Brent before Riley does.

 *Tara*

LUNCHTIME WITH THE GIRLS IS AWKWARD. WHITNEY Blaire is brooding about something. It's obviously serious because she's wearing her sunglasses inside and not stealing food off Pinkie's tray. I'm likewise quiet, thinking how Riley is much better company. Pinkie is the only one chatting, pretending that everything is normal.

"You know what we need to do?" Pinkie says. "Sleepover at my house. We rent some girly movies, get some greasy pizza. Have an early start to the weekend. What do you say?"

I shake my head. "I can't, you know I'm in training."

Whitney Blaire grunts. My guess is she's either going to complain that I stick to my diet better than she does or is about to say something about friends being more important than training. Whatever it is she doesn't say it, because Pinkie continues.

"We can get pizza from Gio's. I know they do a whole wheat crust, and all their ingredients are natural."

"We better get a regular one too, and we'll see which one gets eaten first," Whitney Blaire adds.

Pinkie smiles as she assumes all is well in her little henhouse. "And if we start right after school, then you can still get to bed early for your morning run, Tara. It's been ages since we did something just the three of us."

I'm not in the mood for a girls' night. I don't want to hear all about Pinkie's worries or Whitney Blaire's bitchiness. Of course I don't tell them that. "I'd love to, but I don't think I can. I have to hit the gym after school."

Whitney Blaire scowls. "I hope you're not spending more time with that freak kid. I'm telling you, stay away from her. She's evil."

I drop the apologetic attitude. "Lay off Riley. She hasn't done anything to you."

"No, just to you," she growls.

My eyes narrow and I press my lips together. "If you must know, I'm not meeting Riley. I'm spending time with Brent."

Whitney Blaire's voice suddenly changes to sugary sweet. "So you two are back together now?"

I feel my back grow tense. "No, we're just working out. It's no big deal."

Pinkie takes a deep breath. "Tara, are you sure that's a good idea? Getting close to him again? I don't want to see you get hurt."

I roll my eyes. "Nothing's going to happen."

"That's what you think," Whitney Blaire says under her breath.

"What are you talking about?" I demand.

"Nothing. You just go and have fun."

"I will." I grab my bag and take off.

"Stop by my house afterward if you can," Pinkie calls out. "I'll get the pizza."

I keep walking, keep moving. If I walk fast enough maybe I can get around the whole school before the bell rings. No need to tell Pinkie that even though Gio makes a great pizza, I really don't want to hang out with Whitney Blaire at the moment.

Whitney Blaire

I KNOW I HAVE TO FOLLOW RILEY AFTER SCHOOL. OR AT least get to the gym by four thirty. I still don't know exactly what the plan is and how I'm going to stop it, but it doesn't matter. I can lie my way through anything. And I'm good at thinking on the spot.

The only problem is that the gym is far away. I need to drive there. But I still haven't passed the stupid test to get my license. Pink usually drives me around. She has this loud, clunky old thing that smells like little kids, but as Pink always reminds me, at least it usually runs. But I can't get Pink to drive this time. She wouldn't approve. She'll probably call Riley up and try to sort things out. Like mothers do when their kids are fighting in the playground: "Now children, what seems to be the problem here? Why don't you hug and make it feel better? There, there, good children." Screw that. Pink isn't the only answer to my driving problems. I can find someone else with wheels.

I look around the school parking lot and recognize a kid

from one of my classes. He's unlocking the door of a VW. It isn't a great car, but it's a newer model. I think he is just barely sixteen, but if he can drive, that's all that matters. Shoulders back and swaying my hips, I walk toward him.

He glances my way and then pretends to be looking at something else, yet I know his eyes are on me. I flip my hair, smile, and give him a little wave. His mouth drops a bit. I want him to look behind him to double-check that it's him I'm looking at and not some other random guy, but he doesn't. His eyes stay on me. Which is fine too.

"Hi." I have no idea what his name is, but when you smile as sweetly as I am, names don't matter. "I was wondering, would you mind giving me a ride? See, my friend was going to take me to the gym, you know the one out by Target, but she must have left without me. I really need to work on my . . ." Shit! What is the fitness word for ass muscles? "On my squats. So can you? Give me a lift?"

The guy blinks a couple times. "Ah, sure. Hop in."

I give him another smile. "That's great. You're a lifesaver."

He shrugs me off, but I can tell he's blushing.

I chat with him the whole way to the gym. Don't ask me about what. My mouth might be blabbing away, but my mind is thinking about a plan. A good plan to counteract Riley's bad one, which I still don't have the details on.

I wave good-bye to my ride before he can ask for my number. I walk around the parking lot. I find Riley's skankmobile hiding out by the emergency exits, but there's no sign of Brent's car. That's okay. It isn't four thirty yet. I have to find Riley.

I walk into the gym as if I belong there. I don't stop to pay. Although I can feel the glares of the people working the front desk, no one stops me either. Just goes to show, if you act like you should be doing something, no one questions you.

Now the trick is to find Riley, and hopefully without her or Tara seeing me. Let Tara thank me later when I've saved her relationship with Brent and showed the world the kind of person Riley really is.

The window overlooking the gymnastics area is one of the first things I find. I peer through and spot Riley right away. I can see her perfectly. I put myself behind a cardboard vitamin ad so that if Riley happens to look up, she won't see me through the glass. Ah, this is too easy. I shift the display a bit to get comfortable and watch her.

Any idiot could see she's up to something. Every three seconds, she looks at the big clock on the wall. Even though I can't hear what is going on, I know by the way the coach waves his arms that he's telling her off for not paying attention. At 4:26, Riley goes up to the coach. She puts this pathetic face and I bet anything she's telling the coach that she needs to go to the bathroom. The coach looks at his watch and probably says something like can't it wait. Then Riley goes all apologetic and I can practically hear her saying that it's a female emergency. The coach rolls his eyes and waves her off.

This is it. I have to stop her now. There's just one little problem. I'm a floor above her and I don't know how to get down to the gymnastics door. I see the stairs and take them quickly. My heels echo across the whole building as I clump down the stairs. Shit. This is no way for a sneak counterattack.

Getting them off would take too long. I try running on my toes and that seems to help. I see a door that says GYMNASTICS GYM: TRAINERS AND STUDENTS ONLY. At the end of the hall I see Riley walking toward another door. I can't reach her in time; if I run she'll hear me and get away. There has to be some way to stop her. I look around for something, anything. The fire-alarm box is just a few feet away. I don't know what good it would do, but it's a distraction, and I'm desperate.

I am reaching for the little hammer to break the glass when someone grabs my arm.

 *Tara*

BRENT HAS STOOD ME UP.

I wait a while, until almost five o'clock, and still nothing. Well, forget him. I'm not about to waste the whole afternoon waiting for him to never show up.

On the way out, I glance through the window to the gymnastics area. I don't see Riley. I think about checking the locker room for her, but that seems a bit weird. Besides, it's getting late. Sherman has been locked in the house since early this morning and I have to get dinner started.

I keep an eye out for Brent as I leave. Walking across the parking lot, I see a car that looks like his. I get closer. It is his car. I recognize the bumper sticker the soccer team uses to promote their games: WATCH BOYS PLAYING WITH THEIR BALLS. I've tried to get Brent to remove it, but he won't.

There's someone in the backseat. The windows are fogged up, but I can see the brown form of Brent's head. He must be looking for something. Probably lost his gym pass again. I get closer to knock on the window. That's when I notice the car is shaking, rocking back and forth.

I stand there. The car squeaks as it moves. I can't see inside, but he's not just having a hard time scratching his back. There's someone else in there. I don't know who. The images I have almost managed to repress suddenly stampede into full gallop, but altered. Brent with Someone Else. Someone Else with Brent. I hear a grunt, a moan, and then the car stops shaking.

I turn on my heel then power walk back to the gym. Long, fast strides, as fast as possible without breaking into a run. Control, control yourself, Tara.

I walk right by the front desk. I don't look at anyone and I don't see anything. I don't go to the RTC. I go to the small training room that doesn't have glass walls. No one else's there. I dump my duffel and finally let go.

I hit the four-foot, seventy-pound punching bag. I alternate with each fist. Punch. Punch. Punch. The bag is heavy and it swirls around. I hit it with my hands, my arms, my shoulders, whatever I can hit it with first. I raise my leg and kick the bag. The bag keeps coming back for more and each time I'm there for it. Punch, kick, whatever it takes. I even ram into it with my head. That's a mistake. It swings around and knocks me to the ground.

I roll over on the mats. I get to my hands and knees, but can't manage to get any further. I'm out of breath. My fists are throbbing. My legs are sore. My head hurts. The bag swings above my head.

I stay like that for a while with my eyes squeezed shut. I know I need to pull myself together, get back in control. I know I have to get home. But I don't want to cross the parking lot again.

Whitney Blaire

"JUST WHAT DO YOU THINK YOU'RE DOING, YOUNG lady?"

I swing around to find a security guard holding my wrist. "Quick, sir, there's a fire in the gymnastics area."

"I don't think so. I saw you running down here looking like you were up to no good."

Riley is almost at the door. I'm going to miss her. "That's just it, sir. I saw the smoke from the viewpoint upstairs and rushed down to sound the alarm."

"Well, let's see about that." The guard leads me toward the gymnastics door. I turn around and see Riley go through the other door. I try to yank my arm out, but the guard has a tight grip. Crap. I have no idea where Riley has gone. Off to get together with Brent, no doubt. We enter the gymnastics area. Without looking at the clock on the wall, I know it's just after four thirty.

The coach looks at us. "Does there seem to be a problem?"

The guard places his free hand on his belt to pretend he's

packing. "There was a report of some smoke in here. Do you know anything about a fire?"

The coach looks around. "There's no fire here."

"Sorry to bother you." The guard nods and drags me out. Once back in the main gym area, he squeezes my arm tighter. "So what do you have to say for yourself?"

His grip really hurts, but I don't care about that right now. I look toward the door Riley had gone through. Is there even the slightest chance that I can still stop her evil plan to seduce Brent? "Look, I'm sorry. I made a mistake. Can you just let me go now?"

"No. I'm filing a report," he says, his hand still on his belt. "Do you know what you almost did is a criminal offense? False alarms cost tax payers loads of money."

I switch my tone and smile at him. "I really am so sorry. It was a silly mistake. An accident, really. It was good you were there to sort things out with that coach. Tell you the truth, he was a bit scary, but you smoothed everything out. You were great. Thanks so much."

The guard grunts. "Can it. You can't sweet-talk your way out of this one, princess."

We walk back upstairs. Damn Riley and damn this stupid guard holding me. I give my arm another yank. I can't break free.

I dig my heels into the floor. "I demand you let me go. Do you know who my father is? When he hears how you're treating me, he'll have you for abuse, harassment, and possible child molestation. You don't want that on your record now, do you?"

The guard doesn't flinch. "I'm taking you to my boss, and he'll decide what to do about you and your daddy."

"Fine." I glance at the name badge on his shirt. "Franklin. If that's the way you want to play it." I hold my head high and follow him willingly. I feel Franklin the guard no longer knows if he is doing the right thing. Well, I'm not shitting him. No one in this town messes with the Blaires.

 *Tara*

"TARA?"

I look up to see Riley. Her hair hangs like a curtain so I can't see much of her face. I wish I had hair that did that.

"You okay?" Riley asks.

I push myself up from the floor. I'm in control. I'm in control. "Yeah, of course. The bag just knocked me over. I wasn't paying attention."

"What happened?" Riley offers a hand.

I shake my head. The images don't budge. "Nothing really. Just like I said, the stupid bag . . ." I brush off my pants and try to smile. The smile doesn't quite reach my face.

Riley doesn't try to smile back. I know she doesn't believe me but she doesn't push it. "Are you heading home?" she asks.

My breath is still coming out in jagged bursts. "Yeah, I'm late to get dinner started."

"Let me give you a ride."

I think about that. "Where are you parked?"

Riley makes a face. "Around back, by the emergency exits."

I grab my bag. "Okay, let's go."

Riley leads the way out to her car. I follow her with my shoulders back and my head up. I don't look at anyone, just keep my eyes focused straight ahead. I climb into her red Audi TT and silently thank her parents for getting her a car with tinted windows. I stare in the direction of Brent's car. I can't see it, but then again I can't see that far.

"Which way?" she asks.

Part of me wants to tell Riley to circle around the parking lot. She probably would do it and not ask any questions. But I've already seen enough. I'm not Pinkie. I don't doubt everything I see, hear, or think.

"Turn right once you get out."

Other than give Riley directions, I don't say anything on the ride home. And other than clarify my directions, Riley doesn't ask anything.

She pulls into the driveway before I realize it.

"Thanks," I say.

"No problem, anytime."

I nod and wave to her. I'm halfway to the door when I realize she hasn't moved. I turn around. It's like she's waiting to make sure I get in okay.

I take one more step to the door and then turn around again. "Do you want to stay for dinner?"

Riley responds by turning off the engine and getting out of the car.

Whitney Blaire

THE SECURITY GUARD TAKES ME TO THE SURVEILLANCE room. Right away I notice that there is a camera shot of the cardboard vitamin display. And one of the front desk. Great. Now all I need is for one of these stupid Franklin guards to find the tape of me sneaking into the gym and vandalizing the display on top of almost pulling the fire alarm.

I sit down on a rolling chair and wait for the verdict. Franklin talks to another guard who has spent too many hours looking at the security screens with little more than donuts for company. I can't hear what Franklin is saying, but I'm not paying attention either. I have to get out.

There's no way I'm really going to call my father. Calling Mother wouldn't be any better. They probably can't pick me up anyway. Didn't they say something at breakfast about going out for drinks with some of Father's new clients? Could be. There are always clients and extra work to hold them up. Whatever. I can deal with this on my own.

Franklin leaves and Donut Guard looks at me with

powdered sugar on his mustache. I let my lip quiver. My whole face starts contorting. My ribs jolt upward. I sniff.

"There now," Donut Guard says.

That is the cue I'm waiting for. I bury my face in my hands and start crying. "I'm so sorry! I can't believe I was so stupid. I think I saw a cloud of chalk from the gymnasts and must have thought that was smoke. I didn't mean to do anything wrong. I thought I was being a he-he-hero!"

I feel a tissue by my face. I grab it without looking up. Between my sobs, I hear Donut Guard creaking in his chair. I cry harder but make it sound like I'm trying hard to stop.

"There now," he says again. "Don't worry. No harm done. I think old Franklin was just a bit bored, you know? Tell you what, why don't we call up your parents to come get you and we won't tell them anything about what Franklin thinks he saw, okay? After all, you didn't really do anything wrong. How does that sound?"

I sniff a couple times and nod. "Okay, but can I go to the bathroom? To wash up?"

"Sure, do you know where it is?" Donut Guard asks.

Again I nod.

"Do you want me to call your parents while you get yourself together?"

I hang my head low over the piece of paper and scribble our spare line that isn't actually attached to any phone so it will only ring and ring. Then I hurry out of the surveillance room. Once the door closes, I straighten up and look around. Franklin is nowhere. There are also no cameras. But I know that already. I memorized every single angle I saw on the screen while I was in the room. I need to hurry. I have to get out. But the front doors have cameras on them. There has to be another way.

I remember Riley's car parked out by the emergency exits. But where are the emergency exits? I think about where they are outside and where that would be from the inside. Of course, the door Riley had gone through earlier. I hurry back downstairs. I keep my head low, and in the places I know there's a camera, I hug the wall underneath it.

I go through the door and into a staff-only corridor. Straight in front is a door leading outside. An old woman with rainbow hair has it propped open while she smokes. I stop myself from ripping the cigarette out of her hand and taking a drag myself. Instead, I scoot past her, neither of us saying anything.

I stop just outside. This is the emergency exit by Riley's car. Or rather where Riley's car had been. I catch just a glimpse of it driving away. Through the tinted window, I spot Tara looking straight ahead. Riley sees me and waves as she zooms by.

 *Tara*

IT TAKES THREE TRIES TO FIT THE KEY IN THE DOOR TO unlock it. When it finally works, I almost get knocked off my feet as Sherman bursts out of the house like the ferocious dog he thinks he is. Before I can stop him, he's sniffing Riley. Instead of being scared, Riley sits down right there on the pavement and scratches him behind the ears. Sherman takes that as a hint to plant all forty-five pounds of himself on Riley's lap. I'm about to apologize, but Riley doesn't seem to mind.

"He really likes you." I make conversation in my effort to act normal. "My other friends tolerate him, but no one really gets to his level."

Riley continues scratching him. "He's a good boy, aren't you? Aren't you?"

At the second "aren't you," Sherman leaps off Riley and starts running laps around the front yard. Riley pretends to chase him and that just gets him more excited. If it had been any other day, I might have laughed at them running after each other, Sherman with his tongue flapping all over the place and Riley with her hair flying around her. They chase each other for a few minutes until Sherman remembers that he's been locked up in the house all day long. He stops dead and gives Riley a guilty look as he lifts his leg.

I enter the house, letting Riley shut the door behind Sherman. I tell Riley the bathroom's upstairs if she needs it and wave quickly to the downstairs: the small living room by the front door and the kitchen in the back. It's good having Riley here. It's easier to stay calm when there's company. And for some reason it's easier to stay calm when she's around.

I put three sweet potatoes from the batch I baked last night in the oven to warm up and then pour some grains into a pot with water.

"Do you like quinoa?" I ask Riley.

She's petting Sherman again and looks up. "What is it?"

"It's a grain, kind of like amaranth. It's very high in protein and contains lots of essential amino acids."

"Okay, why not."

I set the quinoa on the stove and head toward the fridge to make the salad. I get sidetracked when I notice the light flashing on the answering machine. It's probably Pinkie wondering if I'm coming over to her girls' night. I press PLAY.

"Hey, baby." I freeze at the sound of Brent's voice. "Where are you? Sorry I was late, but why didn't you wait for me? I—" I press the DELETE button long and hard.

The bottles on the door rattle as I jerk the fridge open. I yank out the lettuce, the tomatoes, the bell peppers, and an overripe avocado. I look at the cucumber for a second before tossing it in the trash; it's too soft. I pull out a cutting board and reach for the biggest knife from the magnetic strip. A hand seizes my wrist holding the knife. I look down to see Riley staring up at me. I stare back at her. She doesn't flinch.

"I'll take care of the salad. Why don't you get me a drink?" Firmly, Riley takes the knife out of my hand. I unfold my fingers and let her take it away.

My hands clutch into fists. I can feel the veins in my neck pulsing. Calm down. Stay in control. "What do you want?" I say.

She sets the knife down away from me and washes her hands. Then she grabs a couple lemons from the fruit bowl, cuts them in half, and pushes them toward me. "Some fresh lemonade would be nice, don't you think?"

I relax my hands. "Cut some more and I'll make enough for everyone."

For the next few minutes I squeeze each lemon long and hard. All my attention is taken by extracting every last bit of juicy pulp. By the sixth half, I'm starting to get a grip on things. At least I've managed to control myself.

I turn to Riley. The salad is artistically arranged and she is drizzling it with a vinaigrette she made after rummaging through the cabinets.

I take a deep breath. "Why don't you like Brent?"

Riley keeps quiet, though I know she heard me. Finally, she says, "I don't trust him."

"Why?"

Riley sets the salad on the table. She takes her time adjusting it just right. "I met him when I first moved here and right away I got a bad vibe from him."

I fold my arms across my chest and stare at her. "Did he hit on you?"

"Yeah," she says, nodding, her attention still on her salad.

I close my eyes for a second and then breathe deeply. "And you didn't go for him?"

Riley turns to me and looks like she's about to be sick. "Trust me, he's not my type."

I think about my "type": athletic, good looking, supportive of my training, and makes me happy. I thought that was Brent, but now he only ranks three out of four.

"Besides," Riley continues, "your friend Whitney Blaire made it very clear that he was taken."

I add water and honey to the lemon juice and taste it. My face puckers. I pour myself a sour glass and then add more honey to the rest of it.

"Tara?" Mom calls from the front door. She comes into the kitchen, sees Riley, and smiles.

"Mom, this is Riley," I introduce them as I open the oven. "She's staying for dinner."

Mom gives her a hug. "So, you're the gymnast. Tara talks about you all the time. I'm Linda. I was wondering whose car that was. I thought maybe Brent had gotten a new one."

With a loud crash, the tray of sweet potatoes drops on the floor. Sherman wolfs one down before Mom grabs him by the collar. I pick up the tray. Riley gathers up the hot sweet potatoes and quickly pops them back. With the utmost care and attention, I place the tray on top of the cutting board. Slowly and carefully. Bit by bit, I pick off the debris from the skins. Then I remember to breathe deeply.

"No, Brent still has the same car," I say. I shut the oven door and turn it off. I remove the oven mitts and press against the counter. I turn back to the potatoes. "But you won't be seeing him around here anymore."

Even with my back to Mom and Riley, I can tell they're taking turns looking at each other and looking at me.

"I thought you were going to get back together." Mom tries to place a hand on my shoulder but I move away. "Did something happen?"

I pace up and down the kitchen. Two steps and turn around. My arms tighten around my sides as I rock back and forth. "Yes, but it's fine. I just need to get in shape. Focus on my miles. I'm fine. I don't have time to date. It's fine. Completely fine. It's all for the best. Everything is fine. I really am fine."

Mom wraps her arms around me. At first I try to break away, but Mom doesn't let go and at last I give in. I squeeze my eyes shut as I keep as still as possible. I don't make a sound; I don't cry. I just let my mom hold me until it all goes away and I'm back in control.

At one point Sherman whimpers and paws my leg for attention. That's when I remember Riley is there. She whispers to Sherman to come. I hear his nails against the floor and the sounds of Riley soothing him, comforting him, telling him it's going to be okay.

I take a deep breath and let go. Mom rubs my back before dropping her hands to her side. Then Riley hugs me. Her hug is solid and strong, and feels like it comes from a much bigger person than she is. Whitney Blaire always gives one-arm half hugs like she didn't want to get too close, and Pinkie's hugs are comforting and squishy like squeezing a pillow. But Riley's hug is different. When she holds me it feels safe . . . and nice. But maybe a little too nice.

I turn away and drink some of my sour lemonade. My heart is beating fast. I breathe out slowly. It's okay, I tell myself.

When I look at the table, it's set for the three of us. Mom had washed the sweet potatoes and put one on Riley's plate with some quinoa and divided the other potato between the two of us.

"The salad looks beautiful," Mom praises. Riley glances at me and grins.

We have just finished dinner (I can tell Riley didn't like the quinoa, though she ate it all anyway) when the phone rings. Mom leans over from her chair and picks it up.

"Hello, Brent . . . No, I don't think Tara is here right now." Mom looks at me with her eyebrows raised. I get up and walk over. "Oh wait, here she is."

She hands me the phone.

I take a deep breath. "Hello."

"Ah baby—" he starts, but I cut him off.

"Brent, don't call me 'baby.' And don't call me ever again." I slam the phone on the cradle. Mom and Riley glance at me. I don't say anything, and neither to do they. I clear the table and start running the water into the sink. Riley comes over and dries while I wash. I vaguely notice Mom going out with Sherman as we finish cleaning up. It isn't until we put everything away and wipe down the surfaces that someone finally breaks the silence.

"I better get going," Riley says. "My parents will be wondering where I am."

I point to the phone. "You can call them."

Riley shakes her head. "It's all right. I don't want to worry them more."

I wait for Riley to elaborate, but she doesn't. Fair enough. I don't need to question it. Just like she hadn't questioned me.

 *Pinkie*

NOBODY HAS SHOWN UP FOR OUR GIRLS' NIGHT. STILL, I order a healthy pizza and a regular one as planned. I make sure we have some vegetables in the fridge in case Tara wants to add them to the pizza. Then I call back the greasy pizza company and ask if they can include some regular soda for Whitney Blaire. I know Whitney Blaire prefers diet, but there's no way I'm feeding my friend something that is proven to cause cancer.

It is just after seven when Whitney Blaire knocks.

"Hey," I say as she brushes by me to the kitchen. "I was just going to call you. Where've you been?"

She grabs the bowl of chips and starts munching. "The gym."

I lick my lips. Whitney Blaire knows how much I hate it when she lies to me. And yet she still does it. I sigh and pretend I believe her. "Did you have fun?"

"Why would I?" She continues eating as she stares at the wall. I bring her a slice of pizza and can of soda. She doesn't even look at what kind it is before she takes a big gulp.

"Are you okay?" I ask.

Whitney Blaire suddenly starts poking around as if she's searching for something. Don't know what. Daddy and Barbara are at the neighbors', and before we take over the living room Angela is watching one of her silly teen movies where the leads don't even kiss.

"So, Tara isn't here?" It's a question but she says it more like a statement.

"I'm sure she'll come any minute," I say, even though it's more optimistic than I feel.

"Stupid bitch," Whitney Blaire mumbles as she shovels more food down.

I quickly grab the phone and give Tara's house a call. Her mom answers.

"Hello, Mrs. Hopkins, it's Pinkie. How are you?" I politely make small talk, even though all I want is to know about Tara. I can't help it. It's how Barbara raised me.

Mrs. Hopkins sighs. "We've been better, but I'll let her tell you. I suppose you want to talk to Tara?"

"Yes, please," I say eagerly. What's going on? What's wrong with Tara? Did she get hurt? Is she going to be okay? Maybe we should drive over there. Whitney Blaire has finished the chips and is working her way through the greasy pizza, and not just the slice I gave her.

"Sorry, Pinkie," Mrs. Hopkins says as she returns. "But she's gone to bed already. It's been a hard day for her and we had Riley over for dinner as well. I'll have her call you in the morning, okay?"

"Okay, thanks." I hang up feeling more helpless than before.

Whitney Blaire has stopped eating long enough to stare at me. Her look makes me squirm. "Tara's asleep," I mumble.

"What? It's seven thirty on a Friday night. What's she doing sleeping?"

I start wiping the crumbs from the counter. I decide not to tell her the whole truth. "Mrs. Hopkins said she's had a bad day."

Whitney Blaire throws her empty can in the garbage. But because her aim is bad, she doesn't make it and a little bit of leftover soda splatters on the floor. "Bad day, my ass. I'll give that bitch a bad day."

"Hey, watch it," I scold her. I don't like it when she calls people bad names. It always makes me wonder if she's ever called me the same thing. She's never called Tara that, and I don't see why she would now. Twice. Unless she was talking about someone else, but I don't know who else that could be. "Shh. Angela might hear you."

"Hear what?" Angela calls out from the living room. "Who's a bitch?"

I send Whitney Blaire an evil look, which of course she ignores. She's busy closing the cardboard lid of the pizza box. She places it against her hip and grabs the second can of soda.

"Take me home," she demands.

I frown. Coming from Whitney Blaire, that statement means a lot. "What do you mean? What about our girls' night? I rented five movies—well, four for us and one for Angela, but I'm sure—"

"Are you going to take me or do I have to call a cab?" She

of all the stupid things   117

gives me this look that makes me feel helpless and useless, and that hurts. Whitney Blaire has always had a way of twisting emotions to make me feel like the guilty party. I sigh and grab my keys, phone, and purse. As much as I love Whitney Blaire, there are times I wish Tara had left her up in that tree.

Our girls' night ends up with me watching the cheesy teen movie for the millionth time with Angela. The healthy pizza really isn't that bad if you dip the crust in some ranch dressing.

I keep the phone with me just in case, but no one (Tara, Whitney Blaire, and unfortunately not even Nash) calls. Maybe I'll call him later. Right after the girl in the film doesn't get kissed by the boy.

 *Tara*

MOM IS DRINKING YERBA MATE TEA WHEN I GET UP EARLY
on Sunday for my long run.

"Why don't we hit the trails today?" she says. "We haven't
been to the national forest in years."

I don't saying anything and Mom continues. "Sherman is
getting stir-crazy in this house. It'll be good to get out."

I look over at Sherman. He's pretending to be asleep but
his tail wags when his name is mentioned. I nod. "You're right.
He could use a day out."

"Good. I'll pack a picnic and we'll make a day of it. Oh, and
there's a message from Pinkie. She called again last night."

I'm not surprised. I haven't talked to her for a couple days
and her mother-hen radar must be going off. But on the other
hand, I'm not in the mood to deal with her smothering. "I'll call
her later," I say.

I go back to my room to grab a fleece and change my
sneakers for a pair that are better for rough terrain. Back in
the kitchen, I add an extra scoop of protein powder to my

breakfast smoothie. Mom left an ounce of wheatgrass juice for me on the counter. I drink that down while the bananas whirl around in the blender. I pour the smoothie into a bowl and sprinkle some granola for a nice crunch. I finish eating just as Mom packs up the picnic (she made chicken and veggie wraps). We load up Sherman (who started lapping around the house when I pulled out the leash), grab the food, and head out.

The day is clear and brisk, my favorite running weather. It's still rather early in the morning so there are few people on the road. We make the trip in just under two hours; I remember it taking much longer, but it has been a long time since we've been to the forest. Years, as Mom said.

Sherman jumps out of the back as soon as we open the door for him. He goes straight for the squirrels, chasing and barking at them to come down from the tree and play with him.

I look around as I start my warm-up stretches. The leaves are just starting to change colors. There are only a couple of vehicles in the parking lot: a beat-up cream pickup and what looks like a rented blue car. It's good to have a change of scenery. Get away from the house and the town with its people. It's like we've entered a different world; I've forgotten how nice it is.

"It's a shame we haven't come down in a while," Mom reads my mind.

"Yes, it is."

We watch Sherman for a few minutes. The only things he's thinking about are the squirrels, and maybe the tree that's keeping him from getting them, but he's happy nonetheless.

We don't say anything. No point bringing up the past. Or the present.

"Right then," Mom sighs. "What trail are you going to take?"

I look at the trail head. "I don't remember the White Lakes trail being too steep and it's about the right distance—fifteen miles."

"Should we picnic at the lake then once you're done?" Mom asks.

I meet her eyes. Other than our height, the hazel eyes are the only thing we have physically in common. I do want to eat by the lake, but I hadn't wanted to suggest it. I didn't think Mom would agree to it. "Sure, if you want to."

Mom puts a hand on my shoulder and squeezes. "It's our favorite place. There's no reason we should avoid it."

"Okay." I nod my head a few too many times. "I should be done by noon."

"Be careful on the loose gravel," Mom warns.

I nod again as I straighten up. "I will. Hold Sherman so he doesn't follow me."

I get my water bottle, set my stopwatch and pedometer, and take off. I keep my eye on the trail ahead so I'm able to avoid any rocks on the path. It's beautiful this time of year. And peaceful. For the first time in weeks I feel my head clear completely and enjoy the surroundings.

The tall, thick trees envelop me as I run by. A couple times I turn a corner and surprise the squirrels and birds that are on the path. Once I come across two people with frame backpacks, but other than that, there's no one along the trail. I feel like I'm alone, with nothing but the trees and the dirt pounding under my shoes, and it's great. I feel like I can run forever. Not because I have to, but because I want to.

I don't remember specifics of the trail but as I pass certain landmarks, memories come rushing back, and they're not as painful as I would have thought. There's the rock that looks like Pride Rock from *The Lion King*. I remember standing on top of it on all fours and roaring across the plains that seemed to stretch for miles around. Now the rock is barely a couple of feet above my head and what I thought were plains is just a campsite clearing. There's the tree that was almost completely uprooted in a storm but stayed alive (and it still is). I remember balancing along the trunk and pretending that it was upright and that I was actually walking up a tree.

And then I pass the meadow that holds the clearest memory of him in the forest. We had planned to set camp there, but there had been a herd of deer grazing. He motioned to me to be quiet and we crouched down to watch them. I was probably around seven or eight and I wanted to go pet them, but he said if I moved I would scare them away. After a few minutes I got restless. I crept toward them anyway, staying close to the ground. I was just a few feet away when a fawn noticed me. It snorted and the whole herd perked up and bolted. I remember how I sprinted after them, trying to catch up with them, but they were gone within seconds. I got angry when he laughed at me. But then he promised to help me became fast enough to keep up with the deer.

I sigh and feel my pace slow down just a bit. He was so good at making promises; it was keeping them that he couldn't be bothered with. It doesn't bug me as much as it used to. Maybe I'm finally beginning to accept that I can't change what he did to me, to us. And maybe, just maybe, I'm better off without him. And maybe without Brent as well.

I take the last mile to the lake easy, partly to cool down and partly to enjoy the last bit of my run. It went by fast. I don't feel like I ran fifteen miles, but my watch and pedometer say I have. I'm tired, but not as tired as I should be after a fifteen-mile run. I slow down to a walk when I see a family at our favorite spot near an old tree. Then I stop completely to watch them. My heart beats faster than it had been a few minutes ago. I squeeze my water bottle hard. I know them. Well, at least one of them.

The mom is dark and pretty. She looks Native American. No, more like South American. She laughs as she watches the other two people. The little boy, about four, is a lighter version of his mom. He kicks a soccer ball to the man while the man pretends he can't keep up with the ball. The man's beard is graying but what's left of his beard is still the same color as my hair. They look like a perfect family. Happy. But I'm sure it looked the same back when it'd been me kicking the soccer ball.

Sherman bounces up to me then, slobbering all over my running tights. I turn quickly to see Mom coming up another trail. I'm about to suggest to her that we eat somewhere else. But she's already seen the family.

"Kenny?" Mom gasps as she leans against a tree for support.

The man turns and blinks at us. "Linda! And wait, is that Tara? I can't believe it. How are you?"

I don't answer. My lips are pressed together; the veins in my neck show how tense I am. I focus hard on taking deep breaths. I'm not losing control again.

The man jogs toward us. He slows to a walk and stops a

few feet away from me. He reaches out to hug me. I move back a few steps. He looks at me and I stare right back at him.

He runs his fingers through his beard. "Wow, look at you, all grown up. I wouldn't have recognized you. You all right? Life treating you good?"

I stay quiet. I stay still. Only my lungs move: in and out, in and out.

"Kenny, what are you doing here? I thought you weren't coming back." Mom holds on to Sherman's collar. He licks her. I move over to them and place my hand on his head, rubbing his ear. Sherman gives us a doggie smile that shows all his teeth. The man steps away.

"Well, Maria Rosa wanted to see the country." He gestures to the woman. "And we couldn't come all this way and not visit my favorite lake. But really, what are the odds that you would be here too?"

Mom's arm wraps around her rib cage while the other hand continues holding Sherman. Through her jacket, I notice she didn't even bother putting on a bra this morning. "What are the odds indeed."

The woman and boy come over with curious looks. I stare at the boy. He hides behind his mom's legs. I still don't say anything, just continue petting Sherman.

The man looks from the woman and boy to Mom and me. "Ah, Linda, Tara, this is Maria Rosa and our son, José Antonio."

I cringe when he says "our," although I already knew. Then he turns to the woman and speaks to her. I understand enough Spanish to know he says: "This is Linda and my daughter, Tara."

 *Pinkie*

I HAVEN'T SEEN OR HEARD FROM TARA IN A FEW DAYS.

Yesterday David and I were busy all day with a church event. I left a message for Tara, and then called some classmates about homework assignments. When I got off the phone, Tara still hadn't returned my call. But it was late and she was probably in bed already. I pretend not to worry.

Today, Tara still hasn't called. She isn't like Nash; she knows how to operate a phone and is usually pretty good about it. (Still no word from Nash, and I've left him two more messages. I'm trying very hard not to obsess about it.) I leave another message for Tara since she probably hasn't gotten the first one. Her machine is the only one I know that still uses a cassette to record messages. It's probably faulty and deleting the messages or taping over them. I tell myself again that I shouldn't be so obsessive and that there's still not really an absolute reason to worry.

 *Tara*

I STARE AT THE LITTLE BOY. IT'S THE ONLY CHOICE SINCE I don't want to look at any of the grown-ups. He scrunches his face and sticks his tongue out at me. My lips twitch. I'm about to stick my tongue right back at him, but I don't. That would mean that I accept him. Accept who he is. And I don't. Not by a long shot.

I look for familiar things in him. At first I don't see any. He is dark. He has stubby legs. He's three or four years old. There are no similarities.

But that's not true. His hair is dark but fine. His legs are stubby but strong. His face is long just like his dad's, and just like mine.

He moves slightly away from his mom and shows me his hand. Twisting his thumb back, he pushes it all the way to his wrist. I haven't done that trick in years, but I have to see if I can still do it. I can.

The boy smiles at me. Again my lips twitch, but they don't go any farther than that.

I can't look at him anymore, so I turn to Mom. She is still holding on to Sherman. He whines for her to let him go, but she doesn't. Maybe she remembers that as long as she holds Sherman, the man won't get too near.

My hand likewise stays on Sherman as I focus on the conversation.

"Why didn't you tell us you had a new family?" Mom places her free hand on her hip.

The man throws his hands up in the air and shakes his head. When it's clear he has nothing for his defense, Mom continues. "I guess as often as you call and write, it's hard to remember what we know."

The man lowers his voice. "Linda, don't be like that."

Mom responds by raising hers. "Like what? Outraged that you left us without a trace, only to start again in a new hemisphere?"

The man glances at his new family. The little boy is playing with the soccer ball again, but the woman is watching the conversation. I guess she doesn't understand the words but does get the gist of what's happening.

"You haven't changed, Linda. You still put the blame where it doesn't belong."

Mom's face reddens as she hisses. "I'm not the one who left."

The man snaps back. "Well, someone had to. That relationship was going downhill and you know it."

"And the solution was to bail? What about Tara?"

I breathe in and out in jagged bursts. I try to send her a telepathic plea not to bring me into this. But either she doesn't get the message or she chooses to ignore it.

"Did your responsibility for her go downhill too?" Mom continues. "That's what bothers me the most. That you didn't even think about her; you didn't think how hard it would be for her to wake up and hear that you were gone. Do you realize that, for some unknown reason, you were her idol, her superdad, and you abandoned her?"

Stop, Mom, please stop. I can't be in the middle of this. He doesn't need to know these things. Just stop talking about me. But I only say these things in my head because I still can't speak for myself.

"Tara." The man reaches out for me. I'm not staring at him, but I'm not ignoring him either. It's like I'm pretending he's not there, even though I'm looking right at him.

He takes another step, but I just slide closer to Mom and Sherman.

He sighs and backs away. "Tara, you've got to know I didn't want to leave you. I thought of coming back many times just to see you."

I don't say anything. Mom says it for me. "What a bunch of lies. If you cared for her half as much as you say you do, you would have at least tried. You could have kept in touch more often. You could have at least remembered her birthday back in September."

"Oh, right. Sorry about that. Here, just hold on a second." The man trots over to his frame backpack. It's not the same backpack he used when he left us. That old backpack had been huge. I must have been close to ten when I could no longer squeeze into it. I want to ask if he still has that old backpack, but I don't.

He comes back a few minutes later. "I saw this a couple days ago and it made me think about you. I didn't know whether to send it or maybe stop by and give it to you myself. Anyway, here you go."

Walking a big circle around and keeping his eye on Sherman, he stretches as far as he can to hand me a yellow envelope. I take it without thinking. The edges are bent and dirty. I try to open it without tearing it. It breaks across the top and along the flap. I take the card out. It has a picture of a curvy cartoon girl wearing lots of makeup, a bra top, a miniskirt, and ridiculously high heels. The lettering on the card is in glitter and says SWEET 16 TO MY SWEET GIRL!!

I open the card. A twenty-dollar bill flutters out. I don't pick it up. Inside, he wrote: *Tara, thought you might want to get yourself something nice with the money. It's hard to believe that you're already 16! Time sure flies. I think about you all the time. Hopefully I can see you again sometime soon. Lots of love, Dad.*

I try to put the card back in envelope quickly, but apparently Mom read the whole thing over my shoulder.

"Sweet sixteen? Oh, good one, Kenny. Time really does fly. So fast that you skipped a year. Tara's seventeen."

Sherman suddenly breaks free.

"Back off!" the man screams as he leaps to the side. Sherman doesn't even notice. He's much more interested in chasing the ducks that landed on the lake, but too chicken to actually get in the water after them.

The man keeps an eye on Sherman as he barks up and down the lake. "Tara, look, I'm sorry. I . . . you know I've never been any good remembering dates."

I know. I remember the county soccer championship when I was nine. I scored four goals that game, two of them by faking left as he had shown me. But he hadn't seen me score. He had forgotten the game was that day.

He continues. "But you've got to know how much you still mean to me. You're my little girl."

I still don't say anything.

The man sighs and looks at his watch. The woman looks at hers and nods. Making sure that Sherman is still far away, he goes over and kisses Mom on the cheek.

"Linda, we've got to get going. Tara, good seeing you again." He comes up to me. I move away when he tries to kiss me. He sighs and holds out his hand. I shake it hard. The man half smiles. "Still got a good grip on you."

He walks back to his new family. He whispers some things to the mom but I don't understand them. She says something back, looks at us and then down at her son.

I look at him one last time.

The twenty I had dropped earlier is in the boy's hand. Between gestures and the Spanish I learned at school, I can tell that the woman is asking him to give it back to me. He doesn't want to but he does anyway. I take it from him. Jackson's face stares at me for a second before I tear it in half. I hand the little boy a piece. He smiles and I kind of do the same. Now we each have one.

With one more final look, we turn to leave. Mom whistles for Sherman to come as we head up the trail that leads back to the cars.

"I can't believe that," Mom starts as soon as we are out of sight. "That two-faced twit. Leaving us because we were tying him down and then goes off and starts a whole new family. Then has the *nerve* to come back here with *her*, to *our* lake. I bet he wasn't even going to let us know he was back in the country. And then to give you that outrageous birthday card, it's like he never even knew you. To top it off, he can't even remember how old you are! That's what really did it. I just can't believe him. Such a hypocrite. We're so much better off without him."

I nod. Mom keeps on ranting the whole way to the car. I don't say anything. I don't need to. Mom's speaking for the both of us. She flings the uneaten picnic in the trash can, complete with the picnic basket. Even Sherman behaves and gets in the car without chatting to the squirrels first. Mom floors the gas pedal and a cloud of dust flies behind us.

"I could do with a real stiff drink right now," she says as she takes the corners a bit too fast. "Or some really greasy and gooey food." She takes her eyes off the road to glance at me. "I think there's a Burger King up ahead."

For the first time since we found the family by the lake I speak. "Let's go."

# Pinkie

TARA ISN'T AT SCHOOL ON MONDAY SO I FIGURE SHE must be sick. It's those crazy early-morning runs, I know it. It can't be healthy to work up such a sweat when it's getting cold outside. I call her again and ask if she wants me to bring her some chicken noodle soup. No answer. I stop by her house, but no one's home. I try very hard not to obsess, but I still blame myself for not getting her a cell phone for her birthday.

Tuesday I begin to panic. It isn't like Tara to ignore me. I call the gym, but the guy at the front desk is new and doesn't know who Tara is. I think about calling Mrs. Hopkins at work, but I can't remember what corporate office she works for. Whitney Blaire doesn't know where Tara is either, but she also implies that she hasn't tried calling her. I know something horrible has happened. Something more than being stuck in bed with a cold, or a broken answering machine.

By Wednesday, I've asked everyone in school if they know where Tara is. Well, every one of the two thousand students who I think might know Tara, which I guess isn't that many. And everyone except Riley and Brent. Call me chicken, but they intimidate me. Riley because she's still hanging out with the school weirdos and Brent because he always makes me feel like I'm not pretty enough to talk to him.

But I'm desperate now. No one has heard anything from Tara and I can't leave out anyone who might have any kind of information. Still, I get Whitney Blaire to come with me. Only for moral support, of course.

I spot Brent a few feet ahead on his way to the vending machines. "Excuse me, Brent?"

He turns around. He wonders who's called him while his eyes pass right over me to Whitney Blaire. I gave him a little wave. His eyebrows scrunch together and he squints as he looks at me. I wave more. He glances to see if anyone is watching and waits for me.

I hurry toward him. Then I realize how much I'm bouncing and try shuffling but that looks really weird. I fold my arms across my chest, but then think that Brent might feel like I'm accusing him. I let me arms drop even though they feel stupid hanging at my side.

Brent's eyes dart between me and Whitney Blaire, and then he says, "What's up, Brownie?"

I blush and stare at my bag. "It's Pinkie."

"I know."

"Right," I say, even though I don't know whether he really does. That said, he still makes me feel as if I were the one who made the mistake. I glance at Whitney Blaire for a comeback, a joke, anything to help me out. But she's acting very weird. She's not paying any attention to me or Brent, but keeps running her hand through her hair as if there were an invisible mirror in front of her that's helping her perfect the style.

"So, is that it?" Brent asks.

I'm about to say is *what* it, but then I realize he thinks I'm done talking to him. "No, sorry, I just wanted to know, and since I've asked everyone else, well I wonder if you know where Tara is?"

Brent's face scrunches to a scowl. "Why would I know anything about her?"

I shift my bag from one shoulder to the other. Whitney Blaire's still primping and therefore no help. "Well, it's just that I know you're . . . well, you know, friends."

Brent looks like he's about to punch something, or someone. I casually slide back. "We *were* friends," he mutters. "You know, she really hurt me when she dumped me last week. But no matter. I'm seeing someone else."

"Who?" Whitney Blaire finally stopped messing with her hair to give Brent her full attention.

No longer angry, Brent half smiles. He looks sideways at Whitney Blaire. "New girl, long dark hair. Maybe you've seen her?"

A loud clatter followed by quick clacks echoes through the hallway. By the time I turn, Whitney Blaire is halfway down the hall, her schoolbag sprawled at my feet. I look the other way and Brent is already gone. Scooping up her bag, I head after Whitney Blaire.

I catch up with her just in time to see her slap Riley across the cheek. The fury in Riley's eyes is vicious as she pounces on

Whitney Blaire. Grabbing Whitney Blaire's hair, Riley yanks down. Whitney Blaire's arms fly as she screams.

"Girls!" I clap my hands. "Stop it right now."

Neither one listens. I shout and clap again. They keep fighting. It's not even clear what they are doing to each other. They're just a bundle of hair, arms, and screams.

A crowd forms to watch the spectacle, but no one does anything.

"Somebody do something!" I scream frantically. "They're going to get hurt!"

"Throw water on them," someone yells over the noise.

I dig into my bag and pull out the bottle of Sprite I bought earlier. Shaking it quickly, I open it up and spray the girls.

They both shriek. For a second it looks like they're going to attack me for spraying them, but as soon as they separate, David grabs Whitney Blaire and one of the weirdos holds on to Riley.

I gasp as they straighten up. In Riley's hand is a chunk of hair, but her face is also lined with four scratches, one of which is bleeding. Whitney Blaire, for the first time in the ten years I've known her, is a mess. The hair that looked perfect a few minutes ago now resembles a rat's nest. Her face is red and blotchy. Her shirt is ripped so much that the entire left cup of her Victoria's Secret bra is exposed. I want to hug her and take her to the school nurse, but it's taking all of David's strength to hold her back from attacking Riley again.

"You owe me a new shirt, you skank," Whitney Blaire calls out.

Riley blows the hair out of her eyes. "Bite me, Blaire."

Whitney Blaire lunges forward, but David keeps his grip on her.

"This isn't over, slut," she shouts.

"Whitney Blaire!" I gasp, but no one notices. Everyone is suddenly scattering. The weirdo leads Riley away and David takes Whitney Blaire quickly in the other direction.

"Banshee," David hisses. I glance over my shoulder and sure enough Mrs. Bensche is on her way. I quickly put the Sprite back in my bag and scurry to catch up with them.

We dart through the hallways and finally go into the classroom we use for the Honor Society.

"Are you okay?" I ask Whitney Blaire as soon as it's clear we're not going to get caught. "Are you hurt? Should we take you to the nurse or the first-aid station?"

"No," she grumbles, but accepts the wet wipe I hand her. "That was wrong, spraying us with soda."

"What was that all about?" David asks. He has finally released his grip but has kept an arm around Whitney Blaire's shoulders. "I suddenly get this text saying 'WB Riley catfight.'"

"She started it," Whitney Blaire mumbles. I meet David's eye and slightly shake my head no. "I mean, she's been after Brent from the start. She pretends to be Tara's friend—"

"Tara!" I gasp. I suddenly remember why we were talking to Brent to begin with.

"What about Tara?" David asks.

"She's missing. Tara and her mom. They're gone, vanished. Anything could have happened to them. We have to go to the police." I'm at the door when I realize David and Whitney Blaire are still sitting down.

David leans back on the chair, his arm still around Whitney Blaire. "Are you sure they're not at home?"

"Of course I am." But of course I'm not. They could have come home. They could have been home all along, had the car in the shop, and just didn't feel like answering the phone. "I'm going over again."

"I'll take care of Whitney." David grins.

"No, I'm going too." Whitney Blaire walks over and takes her bag from me.

David gets up slowly and puts his hands in his pockets. "Call me and let me know she's okay."

I wave to him and hurry to the car. I start driving away as fast as I dare without being reckless. When the road opens up a bit, I press the gas to just under 40 mph and hope there aren't any cops around.

I focus hard on the road. I don't want to think about all the bad things that could have happened to Tara: mugged, kidnapped, murdered. When she wasn't at school on Monday, I should have gone straight to the police. What if she's done something tragic? What if her love for Brent was more than she could take? What if she—?

No. I can't think about that. I can't think about what will happen if we get to their house and find Tara dead.

Pinkie, I tell myself. Remember the road. Remember you're driving. I take a deep breath.

I dart quick glances at Whitney Blaire, who is primping in front of a real mirror now. She shifts her clothes and suddenly the ripped shirt looks like a vintage off-the-shoulder top. She ruffles up her hair, showing no evidence of a bald spot. Now it looks intentionally messy, yet sexy. I don't know how she manages it.

I pull up to Tara's house. The car is still missing.

I knock twice and then ring the bell. The sound echoes through the house, sounding eerily loud. Usually the dog starts barking, but maybe he's asleep. Whitney Blaire looks through the window before ringing again. I peer from behind her. Nothing moves inside the house. Whitney Blaire tries the handle. It's locked, of course.

"Let's go around the back." She leads the way as I peek through the windows. We go through the gate and then I watch my steps to make sure I don't step in any dog turds. Whitney Blaire checks the back door. It's locked too.

"There's got to be a key somewhere." She starts looking around, under the flowerpots and some stones. I lift up the doormat. There's a semi-rusted key there. I try it in the lock, and after wiggling it a bit the door opens.

I grab Whitney Blaire's hand. I don't want to go in alone.

"Tara?" I call out from the doorway. I quickly remember to close the door so the dog doesn't get out, but then I realize that the dog wasn't sleeping; there isn't a dog or anyone in the house. There's a bowl in the sink, its contents cemented to the sides. The blender is also in the sink, filled up with dirty water. The film on top is starting to mold. It smells like rotten bananas and milk.

"No one's here." Whitney Blaire points out what I already know. "They've been gone for days."

"But where?" I ask. "Tara would have mentioned if she and her mom were going away, especially since they never go anywhere. Maybe someone died and they rushed off for the funeral? But they obviously thought they would be back soon, or they would have at least rinsed out the blender. She loves that blender. She wouldn't let mold grow on it."

"Breathe, Pink," Whitney Blaire orders.

I take several deep breaths and release them slowly.

A mischievous grin spreads across Whitney Blaire's face. "C'mon, let's look around."

"Whitney Blaire, we really shouldn't. We're breaking and entering." I wring my hands as I frantically look around.

Whitney Blaire raises her eyebrows. "What if I find them upstairs?"

I gulp. I hadn't wanted to think that! But someone has to make sure. Whitney Blaire is already halfway up the stairs. I let her go up by herself. I stay in the kitchen where it's safe, though I'm not sure about that. Maybe they've been kidnapped and are being held for ransom. I know it does sometimes happen in real life. But that doesn't make sense. Kidnappers go for rich people, don't they? I don't know what Mrs. Hopkins earns, but I know it's not much. I don't see any blood, so they weren't abducted. I remind myself that the dog is missing too. Nobody bothers taking a dog hostage, do they?

I look around for something that might give us some clues and notice the answering machine blinking. I hesitate. Somehow, listening to the messages seems more intrusive than entering the house. I don't want to, but I'm freaking out. It's for Tara's sake, I tell myself.

I press PLAY. "Hi Tara, it's me, Pin—" I skip my own message and go on to the next one.

"C'mon, Tara baby, don't be like this. What we've got is something special. I need you, you're my everything. Call me."

I want to delete Brent's message, but I know that's not right. I just hope Tara isn't desperate enough to try and get him back. Maybe that's it. Maybe Tara wants to go back with him and Mrs. Hopkins has taken her away to help clear her mind. I imagine for a second Tara handcuffed to a hotel bed while Mrs. Hopkins keeps the phone out of reach. Then I tell myself to get real. That would be my torture, not Tara's. Tara doesn't care enough about phones to be bothered if she can't call someone.

Another message from me and then the next two let Mrs. Hopkins know she has been preapproved to lower her monthly payments by 33 percent. There's one from a neighbor asking to borrow a candy-making cookbook; I think it's the wrong number. Some woman named Joan left her new address. A few more messages from me (had I really left that many?), and then finally one that says something important.

"Linda, it's Marilyn Dawli. Human Resources informed me that they received a call from you saying that you are taking a few days off. While I understand these are unplanned circumstances, please note that this is not acceptable behavior. Being that it is not a medical emergency and you did not give prior notification, this falls under unexcused absences. Although we are not in any position to dismiss you, please bear in mind that we will discuss this behavior upon your return. If you feel the need to contact me, my number is . . ." I skip to the next one, but there is nothing else important, just more messages from me. (Was I really that obsessive that I had to leave seven messages? At the time I thought it showed concern, but when I listen to them on the machine they seem so desperate.)

I feel bad listening to Mrs. Hopkins's private messages, but at least it calms me down to know that they weren't kidnapped and didn't disappear into thin air. Mrs. Hopkins had at least called to say that she wasn't going to work, so that seems to be all right. I delete four of my messages (three is a good number, right?), but then I leave Tara a new message telling her to call me as soon as she gets in. I mean, I really am worried and I don't want Tara to think that I didn't think about her while she was gone.

I call Whitney Blaire down. I hear her close a cupboard door and I know she was snooping in the medicine cabinet. (I don't know why she bothered. There're only herbal balms, Chinese tinctures, and homeopathic remedies in there.)

"Nothing up here," she says when she makes her way down the stairs.

"I think they got called out of town suddenly. I left a message for Tara to call when they get in."

We take a final look around before I lead the way out. I lock the door and put the key back under the mat.

I start driving toward town when a familiar car passes me going the other direction.

"That's them, that's them." I point.

Whitney Blaire looks behind her. "Quick, turn around."

I look for somewhere to pull into but there's not even an intersection. "I can't yet."

Whitney Blaire suddenly reaches over and yanks the steering wheel up. I scream as the car spins. I slam on the brakes and the car jerks to a stop and then stalls. It takes me a few moments to realize we're okay, the car is okay, but we're right in the middle of the road. Still in shock, I inch our way to the shoulder. I sound like an asthmatic as my breath comes out in bursts.

"Whitney Louise Blaire. Don't you *ever* do that to me again."

She gives me an innocent look, but her eyes are shining

with excitement. "What? At least we're in the right direction now."

"Never. Again." I stare at her long and hard so she knows I'm serious.

She crosses her heart like we did in elementary to promise. "Sorry. Never again."

I take a few more seconds to subdue the massive amount of adrenaline racing through my body before starting off back to Tara's.

They're still in the car when we park on the street in front of the house. They turn to look at us and slowly start getting out of the car. With some of the adrenaline still pumping, I burst toward them.

The dog leaps out of the car and right away I notice he's the only one that's happy. Both Tara and Mrs. Hopkins look like they haven't slept in days. Their clothes are dirty and smell like they have been wearing them for a long time. I wrap Tara in a hug. She hugs me back. Through her coat, I can feel her back muscles and her spine. I pull away. It isn't my imagination. Tara has lost weight, and from the looks of it, so has Mrs. Hopkins. I don't stop myself from hugging her too.

Part of me thinks Whitney Blaire and I should leave. Something awful has happened to them and they probably want to be on their own after being away from home for so many days. But I'm not sure whether they'll be okay alone.

"Thank you, Pinkie, that is very nice of you." Mrs. Hopkins returns the hug and kisses my forehead.

Whitney Blaire puts an arm around Tara in a half hug, which Tara returns in the same way. "So, where've you been?"

"Are you okay?" I ask, looking from Tara to her mom. "We've been so worried."

"Let's go inside. I could do with a strong cup of tea."

"Here, I'll help you with the bags, Mrs. Hopkins." I take the plastic bags from her hands. Glancing in them, I see an empty toothbrush packet, a small bag of dog food, and a Burger King wrapper. I must be seeing things, because unless Burger King has gone healthy, Tara and her mom would never eat there. I don't want to be rude and take a closer look into the bags, so I convince myself I'm just seeing things. I give one bag to Whitney Blaire to carry and right away she takes a peek inside. Tara and Mrs. Hopkins don't even notice. With my empty hand, I squeeze Tara's hand. She turns to me and tries to smile. It doesn't work. She still hasn't said a word.

"Thank you, girls," Mrs. Hopkins says when we get into the house, legally this time, through the front door, and set down the bags. "Tara, you want to put the kettle on?"

Tara does that while Whitney Blaire and I just stand around waiting.

"We ran into Tara's father while we were hiking," Mrs. Hopkins explains.

I gasp. "Oh, Mrs. Hopkins, that must have been horrible."

"It was. And Pinkie, if you insist on not calling me Linda, I would appreciate it if you used my maiden name from now on. De Paul."

"Yes, Ms. De Paul."

She nods, then looks from Whitney Blaire and me to Tara, who has her back to us while waiting for the kettle to boil. "Thank you, girls, for being here. Tara can use good friends right now."

 *Tara*

I WANT THEM TO LEAVE. I WANT THEM TO GO SO THAT I can be alone. I've barely run in the last few days; my body feels anemic. I need to get it back into shape. But I can't. Mom is telling Whitney Blaire and Pinkie everything that happened in the last few days. She mentions how good it is that they are here to support me during this hard time.

But I don't need them. I just want to be alone.

But I can't.

So I sit down at the kitchen table with my tea and bear it. Whitney Blaire puts three spoons of raw sugar in her tea but doesn't drink any of it. Pinkie finishes hers quickly and at one point during the story puts the kettle back on the stove. When it whistles, she pours Mom a new cup. Mom is still talking. Going on about how we spent the last few days sulking in a motel, which we had to smuggle Sherman in and out of because we couldn't afford the extra pet fee. Then she tells them about going to the government offices to see how she can officially file for a divorce without his signature or proof that he's legally married in another country.

"But Ms. De Paul," Pinkie says, "there has to be a way. Why don't you talk to Whitney Blaire's father? He must know of some loophole you can work around."

"Yeah, maybe." Whitney Blaire nods. "Father isn't a divorce lawyer, but he can still offer advice."

Mom rubs Whitney Blaire's shoulder. "That's very kind, but on the way home I thought up a new plan."

Mom stands up and goes upstairs. I want to join her. I want to go to my room and close the door. I want to run out the back door and keep on running. I want to be anywhere but here with Whitney Blaire sending sympathetic looks my way and Pinkie with her arm around me. But I stay where I am and nurse my cold tea.

Mom comes down holding a piece of paper. Whitney Blaire sits up to see what it is.

"This is a copy of my marriage certificate," Mom explains. She goes to the burner and turns it on. The gas flame catches the paper and sets it alight. Mom turns off the burner and rotates the paper as it burns. She walks to the sink and holds it until the last second. It falls into the sink, sizzling as it meets water. Instead of scooping out the ashes, Mom turns on the tap. She lets it run until everything goes down the drain.

"There," she says. "I'm divorced."

The phone rings and everyone except Whitney Blaire jumps. No one moves to answer it, although I can tell Pinkie is really fighting with herself not to. The answering machine clicks on.

"Tara, it's Riley . . ."

I'm out of my seat in an instant. At last, I can get away.

PART TWO

 *Tara*

SINCE MOM AND I SAW DAD AND HIS NEW FAMILY BY
the lake almost two weeks ago, I've been avoiding my friends.
I tell them I need to focus more than ever on my training,
which is true. The marathon is just under a month away, and
with my inconsistent training I don't know how I will ever run
twenty-six miles. But really, I just don't want to be around
Pinkie and Whitney Blaire at the moment.

Pinkie is being more overprotective than normal, which
just makes me want to push her away more. I know she means
well, but it's getting to be too much. She's trying to get me to
call her every morning at five thirty before my run and tell
her exactly where I'm going and how long I think it will take.
Then she wants another call to make sure I make it home; she
won't even wait to see me at school. I'm not having it. I guess
she thinks that with all that's happened in the last weeks,
I'm emotionally disturbed and maybe even suicidal. I am not
emotionally disturbed. Who cares that my ex-boyfriend is a
horny bastard and my dad is a two-faced jackass? I don't need

them. I have more important things in my life going for me. I'm totally fine and in control. And I'm not suicidal.

But Pinkie still nags me to be careful crossing streets and has suddenly become this fitness guru, reminding me to take vitamins and keep hydrated. I know she likes keeping her chicks in order, but I'm ready to leave the nest.

And Whitney Blaire, forget it. I am avoiding her too, but for different reasons. Riley told me about their fight and I think Whitney Blaire's being more shallow and jealous than usual. Every time she passes Riley in the hallways, she claws the air, hisses, or calls her some version of "whore." It's like being in junior high again. I usually don't remember that I'm almost a year older, but by the way she's acting, I feel decades beyond her.

So now I'm spending most of my time with Riley. She's eighteen and a jock, and she doesn't ask me how I am holding up every time I see her. Although I'd be lying if I say I need an excuse to be with her. I don't know what it is, but she makes me happy and nervous in a good way. When I'm with Riley, I don't think about everything that's happened.

She's been giving me rides on and off this week, so I'm not surprised when she pulls up after school in her fancy car.

"Fruit smoothies with energy boosts?" Riley flicks her hair out of her face.

I had told Pinkie a few minutes ago, when she offered me a ride, that I was busy getting more sponsors. Now, I can't think of anyone to approach. "Sure, why not."

Riley smiles and nods for me to get into her car. It's the coldest day so far, nearly 35 degrees, but the sun is out and Riley has the top down. I sprint to the car and vault over the side without opening the door. Riley floors the gas and we peel off laughing. She takes the turns sharper and faster than normal. Part of me thinks I should ask her to slow down. The other part is enjoying it. After all, this is Riley. And when I'm with her, I feel safe.

I turn to look at her and see her hair streaming out behind her. It doesn't matter how many times we've hung out, she always looks amazing with all that beautiful hair.

Riley glances my way as she drives. I can't see her eyes because of the sunglasses, but I know they are smiling.

"What are you thinking?" she asks.

I'm imagining how amazing she would look doing a routine on the uneven bars with her hair flying behind her like a superhero. But I can't tell her that. I turn away instead and say the first thing I can think of. "The sky's so blue, it's such a nice day."

Riley smiles even more. We're at a red light and she gives me her full attention. "Yes, it's very nice."

I can feel her eyes on me, not the sky, as she says it. Keeping my face away, I hope she can't see me blush. I don't even know why I'm blushing. We're talking about the weather. It's supposed to be the neutral boring subject. But I'm blushing as if she had complimented me.

We don't say anything else. At some point Riley starts whistling along with the radio. She's still driving fast. She slides into a parking spot between two trucks and then slams on the brakes, leaving only a couple of inches between her car and the post. She closes the top by pressing a button and then turns to me. "Ready?"

We walk to the juice bar in silence. Before we get to the door, Riley suddenly grabs my arm and pulls me away.

"Don't look now. Your little friend's over there with her boy toy."

Of course I turn around. Sure enough, Whitney Blaire is across the street with David. They are walking away eating ice cream, or probably frozen yogurt with extra fat-free caramel sauce in Whitney Blaire's case. She's pretending to laugh at whatever David's saying, but I can tell her attention is on something else. I turn my head a bit to see what she's looking at. There are a couple college guys goofing off in a parking lot right in front of her, and I bet anything that's what Whitney Blaire's really laughing at.

"She's such a seductress." Riley reads my mind, though I wasn't thinking it so bluntly.

"I feel sorry for David," I say. "He's a nice guy."

Riley puts her hands on her hips and shakes her head. "I don't know what he sees in her. Sure she's pretty, but she only pays attention to the poor boy when there isn't anyone better around to seduce."

This time I come to Whitney Blaire's defense. "She might be a flirt, but she's still a virgin."

"Maybe that's what she's told you, but really watch her. She's ready to jump on anything good looking that comes her way."

I watch her pass the college boys. Although her back's to me, I see her shift her head to the side as she checks them out. The boys stop what they're doing to look at her. Then she shakes her head like she always does when she's secretly laughing and amused, and keeps walking. Her head shifts again and this time I see a man jogging while pushing a stroller. Although he's far away, I can tell he's in his forties, and has the older man/James Bond appeal. Whitney Blaire stops and makes a point of leaning over to admire the baby. Whitney Blaire hates babies. It's all show, but neither the dad nor David seem to notice her real motives. Every guy she passes, young or old, gets checked out. Then she turns the corner and I can't see her anymore. How could I have known her for so long and have never noticed this about her?

Riley continues talking. "I wouldn't be surprised if half the guys at school have gotten a piece of her."

I don't want to think of Whitney Blaire like that. On the other hand, it all makes sense. I wonder if Pinkie knows. Probably not, but I'm not going to tell her.

"Oh, great, what perfect timing."

Riley hadn't needed to say anything. I notice Brent's car as soon as she does. I back up closer to the wall and stare at my fingernails. They are cut to the quick, yet there still seems to be some dirt caught in them.

I remember the message he left on the machine while Mom and I were away. About not being able to be without me. But when I got back to school, I heard he was already with some girl with dark hair.

Even with my head down, I know Riley is staring at Brent's car. "Now there's a car that must be full of her fingerprints."

I look up. "Whose?"

Riley suddenly realizes what she said because she turns away from both the car driving up the street and me. "Sorry, nothing. I was just talking to myself."

My mouth drops. No way. I glance in the direction Whitney

Blaire and David left. No, Riley couldn't have meant who I think she did. I step right in front of her, but she won't look at me.

I lean over to try and meet her eyes. "Are you saying that Whitney Blaire was the one in the car with Brent?"

Riley shifts away and opens the door to the juice bar. "No. All I'm saying is that I saw her at the gym that day."

I wrap my arms around my waist. Short puffs of breath cloud in front of my face. She wouldn't do that. She couldn't. But I can't think of any other reason for Whitney Blaire to be at the gym.

❧ *Whitney Blaire*

I SEE THEM WHIPPING AROUND A CORNER IN HER convertible. It's cold enough to freeze the balls off a polar bear, and still they're driving with the top down. The evil munchkin tramp is laughing and Tara looks like she's having the time of her life. Happier than I've seen her in a very long time.

I take a big spoon of sugar-free Rocky Road and swallow it. The coldness rushes up my head as a nut scratches my throat. I choke. David turns around and slaps my back a couple times.

"You all right?"

"Yeah." I take another spoonful and this time savor it. "It's just brain freeze."

"We can go inside if you're cold."

I glance at the parking lot. I see a blonde head and a black head. In a few seconds, they'll probably see us. I link an arm around David's and lead him away.

"Nah, it's part of the fun." And then to prove it I take another bite and put on a brain-freeze face.

David does the same and I laugh.

That's when I realize they're watching us. I don't look, but I can feel Riley's laser eyes trying to burn a hole in my back. I act like I don't know they're watching. In fact I pretend I'm suddenly the one having the time of my life.

I let out an evil laugh.

David raises his eyebrows. "What is it?"

"Nothing," I say quickly. But I say it with a smile.

David catches on. "Oh, go on, tell me."

"No, it's mean." I stall.

"So?"

I look around quickly for something to make up on the spot. I lower my voice and use my chin to point at a few guys in front of us. "See them over there? Don't you think the one in the blue looks a bit like a Pokémon? With that cheesy grin and his hair sticking up like two ears?"

David snorts. "Nah, Pikachu is much cooler looking."

I force out a laugh. I can still feel the evil munchkin tramp staring at me. Part of me wants to turn around and give her the finger, but that makes her win all over again. I pretend to look at some guy's snot-nosed kid, just so that she won't know that I know she's watching me. I haven't forgotten our catfight, and I'd give anything to find someone that will rip that horrible hair right out of her skull like she did to me. She's won too many times. She's already taken my best friend away. I figured that out when I saw them drive off together that day at the gym.

"Whitney?"

I blink a couple times and realize David is looking at

me. I have no idea what either of us said last. I smile at him, pretending to be half embarrassed.

"Wait, what were we talking about?"

He gives me a playful push and goes on talking. I laugh. I pretend everything is okay. I pretend that we haven't lost Tara to the dark side.

 *Pinkie*

TARA IS DRIFTING AWAY. SHE'S NOT TAKING RIDES WITH me to school. I think she's avoiding us, but when I ask her about it, she pats me on the back and says no. She says she's busy with her training and since Riley is an athlete she can relate to her more at the moment. But Tara has always been an athlete, and that never stopped her from hanging out with us. I almost wish she was still with Brent, because even then, she still found time to be with her friends.

I call out to her between classes. "Tara, wait up."

She stops and waits for me. We walk to our next class together. She doesn't say anything, so I feed her the line I've been practicing. "So you know it's Angela's birthday in a couple days, and she decided, crazy I know, that she wants to try water polo this winter, so I was thinking of getting her some equipment and stuff, you know like a mallet or whatever—"

Tara laughs. "You really don't know anything about water polo, do you?"

She's right, I don't, but I use it to my advantage. "You see? I don't even know where to start. So I thought maybe you can help me. Pick out the things Angela might need."

Tara, still amused, nods. "Well, there's no mallet in water polo, that's for sure—but we can look at some balls or caps. So when do you want to go?"

"Whitney Blaire has detention today, so what about tomorrow?" I answer quickly.

Tara frowns. "I'm busy tomorrow. Why not today? Just because we're going shopping doesn't mean *she* has to join us. It's not like *she'll* buy anything at the sporting goods store."

I look at Tara before I speak. It isn't like her to be so mean, but I let it slide for now. "Of course she doesn't have to join us, but it'll be nice if she does. Remember the last time we went to the sports store and we started playing on the yoga balls, but I kept falling off?" I chuckle, although at the time I had been very embarrassed. Tara doesn't even crack a smile.

"Look, if you want my help, I'm free today. If not, then you two can go by yourselves any other time. Ask for Billy—he'll help you."

Tara heads to the classroom. What have I done wrong? Is it something I've said, because for Tara to act this way is just not right. I take hold of her arm and pull her aside.

"What's going on? Are you and Whitney Blaire fighting again?" I've asked a version of that question many times in the ten years we've been friends. Usually Whitney Blaire says something without thinking and Tara, who really is more sensitive than she likes to pretend, gets upset and doesn't speak to Whitney Blaire for a few days. When I've asked the question before, Tara has always said she was fine and then kept quiet. This time she doesn't.

"Took you long enough to figure it out, didn't it?"

I'm speechless for half a second. "But Tara, what happened?"

Tara walks into the room without saying a word. Now that is more typical Tara behavior.

For the first time in my life, I write and pass a note during class. It's just while we're watching a Spanish cartoon, but it'll be hard to explain if I get caught. *What's going on between you and Tara?* I send it to Whitney Blaire. She scribbles a response that I get back a few seconds later. *beats me. i thnk tht bch hs blakmald hr. wnts da hol wold on hr syd.* I sigh. I should know by now that Whitney Blaire's grudges don't disappear quickly. I write back: *Are you sure you didn't say or do anything that she might have taken the wrong way?*

Ms. Ramirez gives us a suspicious look, but Whitney Blaire smiles innocently as she writes the note. In the darkroom, Ms. Ramirez doesn't notice when Whitney Blaire passes the note under the desk to the person in front. Meanwhile, I'm sweating bullets thinking that Whitney Blaire is about to get her second detention of the day. (The first one was for writing crude stuff on the boys' bathroom wall about Riley. I didn't see it, but I'm sure it involved leaving Riley's number and address.)

The note gets to me a few seconds later. Ms. Ramirez doesn't even look my way. Whitney Blaire once said that I could get away with murder because no one would suspect the "model" student. I'm not so sure about being a model student anymore. After all, I've snuck out of school to go to an amusement park (though that wasn't why I snuck out), I'm practically dating a teacher (if he ever calls me), and now I've started passing notes in class. I read Whitney Blaire's new note: *lnch. w'll gt hr B4 she sits wth da bch.* I crumple the note and wonder if that is the best way to find out why Tara is avoiding us.

I look over at Tara. She seems fine; she's laughing at the cartoon (she doesn't have a TV at home so whenever she sees a show she's glued). Maybe there isn't anything wrong. Maybe I'm just overreacting again. Or more likely still overreacting. Maybe Tara is just having bad PMS. Maybe she's not as over Brent as she pretends she is.

Tara is walking and laughing with Riley when I spot her heading to the cafeteria. They don't have any classes with each other, so I'm surprised that they're already walking together.

I take a deep breath. "Tara, can we talk, please?"

Tara's shoulders drop and she has this expression that says "go on."

I look over at Riley. I try to send her a message that I want a moment alone with Tara. Riley doesn't receive the hint. I turn back to Tara and pretend Riley isn't there.

"Please, Tara, tell me what's going on? Was it something I did? Or Whitney Blaire? Please, because whatever it is, I'm sure we didn't mean it and are really sorry. Tell me why you don't like us anymore."

Tara growls. "It's not you, but why don't you ask *her*?"

I look behind me. There is Whitney Blaire with her arms crossed. "Ask me what?"

Tara steps forward. "Where were you two weeks ago last Friday?"

"Two weeks ago? I was here. At school. What are you getting at?" Whitney Blaire asks.

"Where did you go after school?" Tara specifies.

"Two weeks ago last Friday we were going to have our girls' night," I step in. "But you didn't make it, Tara." But we all know that wasn't the only thing that happened that day. It was also the day Tara caught Brent in the car with someone else. At least, Tara and I knew that's what happened that day. I don't know about Whitney Blaire. She's not good with dates, but I can't say anything at the moment.

"But before going to Pinkie's, you were at my gym. Weren't you?"

For a second I think Tara is going to shove Whitney Blaire in the chest like they do in the movies. Instead she just gets really close.

Whitney Blaire is the tallest of us, and with her heels, she towers over Tara. But Tara is the strongest girl I know.

"Girls, what do you say?" I put a hand on each of their shoulders. "Frozen yogurt for everyone? My treat?"

They both push my hand away. I look over at Riley, but she doesn't say or do anything. If they start fighting, I can't do anything; I don't have a drink in my bag. I wish David were here, but he didn't come to school today.

"*Your* gym?" Whitney Blaire points a finger. "If it wasn't for *my* father, defending the developer in court, *your* gym wouldn't even be there."

Tara shifts a bit closer. Even though she has to look up to meet Whitney Blaire's eyes, she's the one that looks more intimidating. Tara always keeps things under control, but right now, I have never seen her so angry. "I don't know why I even bothered rescuing you from that tree. You're so spoiled, I bet you only did it for attention," Tara says.

"Shut up," Whitney Blaire huffs.

"Girls, please," I plead, but they don't listen.

Tara gets an inch from Whitney Blaire and hisses, "Get out of my face. Go run back to Brent."

Whitney Blaire turns red with confusion. "What's that supposed to mean?"

"Oh, I forgot that with your IQ things need to be spelled out."

I gasp. "Tara!"

"Screw you!" Whitney Blaire says. For a second I think she's talking to me, but then I realize she doesn't even know I'm there. "You don't know anything. You don't know anything about me and you certainly don't know anything about your little backstabbing friend. She's the one you should be mad at."

Tara turns to glance at Riley then goes back to Whitney Blaire. "Riley wasn't the one screwing Brent outside the gym a few weeks ago. I know it was you."

Whitney Blaire steps back.

I can't believe what Tara just said. I don't know what to say, and for the first time since I've known Whitney Blaire, she is also speechless. Tara on the other hand is just getting started.

"I don't know why I didn't see it before." She clenches a fist and her eyes flash. "You've been after him since we started high school, and yet you always claimed he wasn't your type. I remember how you screamed when we started going out. I thought you were happy for me, but now I realize you were jealous. That's all you've ever been. Jealous of everyone that's prettier, smarter, and richer. Or dating a hotter guy than you.

And then the second there's a rumor of him doing something wrong, you're the first one to tell me. I bet you were real pleased then, thinking that you could finally have him in your clutches." Tara pushes Whitney Blaire in the shoulder. Whitney Blaire just stares at her.

I want to put an arm around Tara to calm her down, but she is ranting like I've never seen her rant. In fact, she is hysterical and out of control. And she scares me.

"But now you can be real happy. Because I'm never going back to that asshole again, and I'm certainly never hanging out with you anymore. Go cry on his shoulder if I've hurt your feelings. Go make wild passionate love or whatever it is you call it. You deserve a guy like Brent."

There are tears in Whitney Blaire's eyes, but she looks just as angry as Tara. "You have no idea what I've gone through for you, you bitch," she says to Tara, and then turns to Riley. "I was right about you. I know you planned all this, turning Tara against me. Stay the hell away from me and the rest of my friends." And Whitney Blaire bumps against Riley and then walks away quickly, her heels clacking down the hall.

I look from Tara and Riley to where Whitney Blaire has taken off.

"Oh, Tara, how could you?" I ask. Tara and Riley stare back at me, neither of their faces changing expression. I shake my head and take off after Whitney Blaire.

Whitney Blaire

IT DOESN'T TAKE LONG FOR PINK TO FIND ME AT THE SIDE of the school building. Not that I'm running away or hiding. I just couldn't take that smug look on Riley the Bitch's face anymore. As much as I had tried to warn Tara, Riley still wormed her way in. I don't know how she did it. She's only been here about a month and still has managed to turn everything upside down. And now she's got Tara against me too. How? Why? What is it about Riley that has Tara believing her instead of me? Think, think.

Pink tries to hug me, but I push her away. I need to keep moving. There's something that I'm not getting. If I have to wear down the ground by pacing, I'm going to figure it out. Pink sits down with her knees to her chest, watching me. I wipe my face with my arm.

"I'm sorry about that," she says.

"What? It wasn't your fault."

"I know, but still. Tara shouldn't have said those mean things or made those assumptions. I don't know what got into her."

"I do." I break off a tree branch. I hate trees. Ever since I got stuck up that one years ago. I fling the branch as hard as I can. It lands just a few feet away. "It's *her*. Always her. I just wish I knew how she was doing it."

Pink rambles on. "It's not like Tara to lose control like that. I don't think she's eating right. There must be some sort of chemical imbalance, some nutritional deficiency. Tara's always been the calm one, the one in control. What could have happened to make her go at you like that?"

I stop pacing. At first I push the thought away but it comes back. I remember all the looks Riley threw Brent, all the excuses she used to spend time with Tara. I had it all wrong. It wasn't Brent she was after.

"Oh, that Riley," I growl.

Pink tries to be patient. "Yes, Whitney Blaire, you've said it already. I've heard all about how she's the devil's spawn and how—"

I hold my hand up for her to stop. "No, I mean it's because of Riley that Tara—argh, it's so obvious!"

Pink hands me a tissue. "What's so obvious?"

I stare at her but ignore the offer. For someone who's an A student, it sure takes her some time to get it.

"Think, Pink. Who do you choose to believe over your friends?"

Pink squints. "Family?"

I roll my eyes. "Other than family."

"I don't know," she whines. "Just tell me. You know how I hate it when you keep things all secretive like that."

"Come on, Pink, I know you can do it. If you have to choose

between friends and the other important person in your life, the other person is . . . ?"

Pink shakes her head. Then her eyes suddenly widen. "What, you mean a boyfriend? But how does that relate to Tara and Riley? Unless . . . No way. You can't be thinking that Tara and Riley are . . ."

I nod.

"No, no. That can't be true. Tara isn't . . . I mean, they aren't . . . No, they're friends. Seriously, Whitney Blaire, they're just friends. Good. Friends." Pink starts hyperventilating. Not that I know exactly what hyperventilating is, but I guess it has something to do with being twitchy and letting out steam, which is exactly what Pink's doing.

"Good friends, my ass." I fold my arms over my chest. "You don't turn your back on your lifelong friends for someone else unless you're *with* that person."

Pink puts her hands over her ears. "Stop it. It's not true. I mean, Tara was with Brent for months. She's not . . . And Riley, she can't be . . . I mean, she's so pretty."

"*Argh!!!*" I grab another branch and try to snap it. It bends, but doesn't break. I pull it and end up just shaking the whole tree. A bucket of leaves drops on top of me. The branch still doesn't break. Stupid tree. I kick it. It hurts like hell and worse yet, the tree ruins my shoe. I kick it again. "Will you shut up about Riley's looks? First David, then Tara, and now you. I can't take it anymore."

Pink forgets her hyperventilating to wrap me in a hug. I push her away again. "Whitney Blaire, please. I'm sorry. I didn't mean anything by what I said. I just . . . it's hard for me to believe this, if it's true."

I take a deep breath and finally let Pink keep an arm around me. "Of course it's true. Tara's been in love with that bitch from the start."

"I still don't think so."

I push her arm off. "Well, I know I'm right. They're together. Now the question is, whose side are you on?"

"I don't—"

I start walking away. It's time to leave school. "You have my number."

Pink catches up. "Wait, you can't make me do this."

I glare at her. "I'm not making you do anything. I'm just saying that I'm not hanging around people that hang out with that bitch. Tara's made her choice. Now it's your turn. I'm out of here."

"Whitney Blaire, wait." Pink stops. "You can't go. You have detention."

I keep walking. "Call me when you've made up your mind."

I shake my head and shift my purse. I give her two hours. Three at the most.

 *Pinkie*

I GO THROUGH MY AFTERNOON CLASSES WITHOUT knowing what I'm doing. I write down everything the teachers say, but I don't hear a word of it. By last period, I can't take it anymore. I have to leave. I am only missing PE, a pass/fail class. And knowing the people who've passed that class before, I think it's okay to miss one class. I can't focus on gym right now. The last thing I want to worry about today is yellow balls aimed at my face.

How could Whitney Blaire do this to me? How can she make me choose between her and Tara? And if what Whitney Blaire said is true, how could Tara do this to me? I don't know which one is worse: Whitney Blaire telling me to choose between my friends or Whitney Blaire telling me that she thinks Tara and Riley are a . . . are doing . . . No, I can't even think about that. It is too gross. I mean, what if Tara has always been that way? Oh my God! I've changed clothes around her. We've joked around about my bouncing monsters. What if she was checking me out? And that day we were joking about spying on Nash, she said I should go in drag. Did that mean something else? Like she had a crush on me? Oh God, oh God, oh God.

I pull over to the side of the road because I can't drive and drive myself crazy at the same time. Breathe, Pinkie, breathe. Inhale, exhale. Okay, now think of something else. Think about something that doesn't have anything to do with Tara possibly being . . . Don't think about Tara, and Tara and Riley together. Think of something else, someone else. Whitney Blaire saying it was her or Tara. No, no stop it. Don't think about that either. You can't possibly choose. It's stupid. There's no choice to make. You're not going to choose Tara now that she's a . . . But on the other hand, it's really shallow of Whitney Blaire to even suggest that you should choose between them, so that's not the right choice either. There's no one to turn to. My best friends have abandoned me. I need to talk to someone. I can't do this on my own.

I pull out my phone. Who can I talk to? Mama. No, I need someone who will talk back. There has to be someone else.

A car horn beeps. I look around me. I'm not exactly on the road, but since there isn't much of a shoulder, I'm not actually off the road either. I wave apologetically at the guy who beeped at me. He gives me the finger. I need to get off the road, but I don't want to drive. Okay, where am I? I recognize the street and put the car into gear. Ninety-six seconds later, I pull into David's driveway. I ring the bell. Please be home, please don't be so sick you're under quarantine.

His youngest sister, Carolyn, answers the door. Her face is covered with blue eye shadow and red lipstick, but not necessarily in the right places.

"David," she shouts. "Your girlfriend is here."

"I'm not his girlfriend," I mumble.

Three seconds later, I hear thundering from upstairs and then the thumping of stairs being taken quickly. When David sees me his face changes from excited to surprised. "Oh, it's you, Pink. Why aren't you at school? Are you okay?"

"No." I start crying. I fall into his arms and he lets me hug him without breaking away.

"Eww, smoochy, smoochy," Carolyn says. I can feel her watching us, even though my eyes are closed.

"Beat it, Carolyn, or I'll tell Sophie you've been in her room."

Carolyn stomps away. David rubs my back and I hold on tighter.

I pull away from David as soon as my nose starts running. It's one thing to wet his shirt with tears; it is something else to get snot all over it. I take myself to the bathroom and blow my nose. I grab some extra tissues and stuff them in my pocket. Okay, Pinkie. Pull yourself together. I wash my face and make the mistake of looking in the mirror. Oh, great. Creature from the black lagoon with blotchy red skin. Oh, what does it matter, it's just David. Still, I run a hand through my hair before coming out and hope it helped just a bit.

David is waiting for me. "Better?"

I nod. "Yeah. I'm sorry, I just lost it. I guess I need someone to talk to."

David grabs his coat. "Let's go for a walk."

"You're not sick? You weren't at school."

"It was just a headache. It was gone when I woke up again a few hours ago. Let's go."

I nod again and follow him out. The second the door closes

behind us, I let it all out. "Tara and Whitney Blaire had a big fight at school where Tara falsely accused Whitney Blaire of having an affair with Brent because of something that Riley said, so that got Whitney Blaire all angry and now she wants me to choose who I want to be friends with, but Whitney Blaire also thinks that Tara is now a lesbian in a relationship with Riley."

David lets out a whistle. "Damn."

"And I don't know what to do or what to think."

David blinks a few times. "So, Tara and Riley? That's big."

I shake my head. "I don't believe it. I mean, Whitney Blaire has no proof. She just assumed that since Tara took Riley's side in believing something untrue about Whitney Blaire, that they're a couple. But it can't be true."

"Why not?"

"Because it just can't be—it doesn't make sense. Tara dated Brent for months, and she went out with other guys before him. And it's just wrong."

David takes my hand and gives it a squeeze. "It's not wrong. You just didn't expect it to happen to a close friend."

I sniff and pull out a tissue. "That's just it, Tara's not the sort. I think this is just another of Whitney Blaire's dramas. Her imagination working overtime."

David stops walking to look at me. "If you really thought it wasn't true, would you be so upset?"

"I—" I stop. I force myself to really think about it. The looks Tara sent Riley from across the room, the eagerness to spend as much time with her as possible, and the giddy smile on Tara's face when they were together all come to mind. I suppose it could be true, or at the very least possible. "You're right. I just don't want to believe it. It's such a shock."

We start walking again, his hand still holding mine. "It is, but we still should have seen it coming. They have so much in common, always at the gym together. Anyway, I bet Riley's gay."

I look up at him. "What makes you say that?"

David shrugs as if he knows a secret. "Pinkie, I'm a guy. It's what makes her so hot—but don't you dare tell Whitney I just said Riley was hot. Besides, it's all in Riley's signals. And, she looks gay."

I pull my hand out of David's and stare at him. "Are we talking about the same Riley looking like a lesbian? Because the one I'm talking about could win Miss America if she were taller—though if you tell Whitney Blaire that, *I* will hurt *you*."

"I didn't mean like diesel-dyke gay. It's just there's something about her, about the way she acts. Look who she always eats lunch with. And she could have any guy in school but isn't interested in any of them. Maybe I'm wrong, but I have been thinking it for a while. Well, fantasizing about it." David grins impishly.

I ignore that comment. I don't understand what it is about boys and lesbians.

"Why didn't you say anything?" I sniff again. David not telling me hurts almost as much as all the other stuff.

David shrugs. "Like I said, it was mostly just in my imagination, though I did convince myself of it. Besides, Whitney hates her so much, I didn't want to bring her name up. And I know you don't like gays."

I shake my head. "I have nothing against gays. I just don't like them near me."

David nods. "I know. And since you girls have these massive makeover slumber parties that all girls are known for, you've seen each other without clothes on."

I think about that. It's not the only thing that bothers me, but it's certainly a part of it. "Well yes, but it's not like we've really looked at each other. Not like that. But if Tara *was* looking at me and I didn't know it . . . Eww, that's just gross."

David gets a guilty smile. "So, how does Whitney look without a shirt on?"

I playfully hit him on the shoulder. "I just told you I don't look. But for the record, she doesn't look any different than the rest of us."

David sighs, but I can't tell if it's a happy sigh or a sad sigh. "Do you think I'll ever have a chance with her?"

"Well, she certainly likes you." I pause for the right way to say that what I think Whitney Blaire really likes is not so much David himself, but rather the admiration she gets from him. "So maybe if you're patient."

David lets out a sarcastic laugh. "I've been after her since that day in first grade when you introduced us. She stuck her tongue out at me and then winked. I don't think I even knew what a wink meant, but it worked."

We walk a bit in silence, David no doubt wondering what he could do to finally win over Whitney Blaire, and me glad that I talked things over with him. I still don't know what to do and how to feel, but at least I feel a bit calmer about it.

David suddenly stops and I see that we have ended up right

in front of the cemetery. I pick up his hand again and squeeze it. "Do you mind if I say hello real quick?"

"Course not. I like cemeteries. They're cool. But I didn't think you would want to."

I lead the way down the path and then to the right. "It's fine. I come here a lot, at least a few times a month."

I take a detour to the pump and fill the watering can the caretaker leaves out. Even though it's November and the marigolds are either dead or on their last leg (which I guess they're not, since marigolds don't have legs), it's a habit I can't give up. David offers to carry the watering can and I let him. Not because it is the guy thing to let him take it but because I know he's trying to help and it's sweet of him to offer.

A few buds still have orange and red petals. I give those the most water, but make sure even the dead ones get a drink. Then I crouch down and speak to her.

"Hi, Mama, it's me Pinkie. I brought David here with me today. He's been great in helping me cheer up. Tara and Whitney Blaire aren't speaking, and I'm stuck in the middle, yet again. The only problem is that I don't know if they will patch things up this time around. They said some pretty bad things to each other, and truthfully, I don't like what either one is doing or saying, so in a way I don't feel like talking to either one at the moment. So no one is talking to anyone right now. It's nice to at least have David to talk to. Thank you for taking that prenatal class with his mama seventeen years ago; he's turned out to be a great friend. I love you and I'll be back soon, probably with Daddy on the anniversary. Don't forget me."

I kiss the air and trace the headstone with my fingertips.

Behind me I hear David reading the engraving. "'Aurora

Pauline Ricci. Beloved wife of Dino and adored mother of Pinkie. At peace.'"

I get back on my feet and take one more look. David stands behind me and wraps his arms around my shoulders. I lean into him just a bit.

"You know, considering we've known each other since forever, I can't remember ever hearing your real name."

I turn to face David. "Who says Pinkie isn't my real name?"

David rolls his eyes. "Come on, you can't expect me to believe your parents named you after a newborn hairless mouse."

I sigh and start walking back to return the watering can. Leave it to David to know exactly what a pinkie is. At least he's not calling me "Snake Food."

"When I was born, Mama said that I looked like a baby mouse, all small, pink, and helpless. She always called me Pinkie, except when she was mad. Being Pinkie is one of the few things I have to remember her by."

"Oh, I'm sorry." He looks down and kicks the dry leaves on the path. "I liked your mom. I remember she gave me an extra popcorn ball on Halloween."

I smile. Mama's popcorn balls were the best: made with homemade buttery caramel and a few peanuts to perfectly balance the sweet-and-salty combination. "That was to make up for the later years with the Blaires not welcoming trick-or-treaters and Tara's mama giving us packets of unsalted sunflower seeds."

David grins mischievously. "I always gave the sunflower seeds to Sophie and told her all the big kids ate them with the shells. Later on she realized that even the birds don't eat the shells. But I think Carolyn still eats them that way."

I chuckle. I never thought of feeding Angela the sunflower seeds Ms. De Paul gave us. Every year I tried to grow them for Mama without any success. Probably because I always planted them in November.

"Those were good times," I say. "It's a shame they won't be the same again."

David drapes an arm over my shoulders. "You really think the friendship's over?"

"I don't know. I'm just fed up with them right now. I'll probably call them in a couple days and do everything I can to get us all back together. Hopefully, they'll forgive each other. But I've never seen them fight like this."

David steps right in front of me. "You know, Pinkie, it's not your responsibility to work things out for everyone. It's not your fault Tara and Whitney are fighting."

I pick up David's hand again. It's a nice thing for him to say. Even if it isn't true.

Whitney Blaire

I EXPECTED TO GET A LECTURE FROM THE PARENTS FOR coming home late last night without calling. I even thought I might be grounded if the school called and told them I missed detention. But there was nothing. When I wake up in the morning, I find out why.

There's a note. I must have missed it last night. It says:

Darling,

I just found out I have to join your father for the conference in San Diego this weekend. I know we were going to see Riverdance, *but there is no way of getting out of it. If you still want to go, call Patrick at the box office. He knows how to charge it to our account—I'll leave his number. I've asked Carmen to stop by on Sunday to check up on you. If you need anything, do give her a call. I'll leave you her number as well, in case you don't have it. I'll be back Monday afternoon. Your father says to remind you to make sure you get to school on time Monday morning.*

Affectionately,
Your Mother

P.S. You may invite your friends over for pizza one night if you are lonely.

Next to the note, there's a fifty instead of the usual twenty. It's a new one, all crisp and sticky. I hold it, rubbing my fingers over the ends to see if there are two stuck together. With the other hand I crumple Mother's note into a tiny ball. Then I stop.

A smile crosses my face. I set down the money and open up the letter carefully. I read the last line again. The smile widens. I press my hand over the note to smooth out the creases. I go upstairs with the two pieces of paper. The money I place in its usual spot in the leather wallet on the top shelf of my closet. The note goes in my sock drawer. If anything goes wrong, I have the proof of permission kept safe. I haven't grown up with a lawyer and a psychologist in the house without learning something.

Back downstairs, I look all over for the school directory. It's not by the phonebook or by any of the other phones around the house. I try Father's office door, but it's locked. With the deadbolt. What a surprise. I guess the school directory wouldn't be there anyway.

I think of calling up Pinkie. I haven't heard from her since yesterday. I know she hasn't taken Tara's side, probably just busy with church or something stupid like that. But I don't call her; I'd have to explain why I need the number. Not a good idea. I'll tell her after everything is planned; when there's no way for her to stop me from doing it. I get my phone out of its case and look through the contacts; there has to be someone who has his number. Actually, I have it myself. No idea how I got it but who cares.

He answers on the fifth ring.

"Hey."

"Gator, it's Whitney Blaire."

"'Sup?"

"Do you still have a band?"

"Yup."

"Cool. Any chance you're free tonight?"

"You paying?"

"Gator, it's a chance for everyone who's anyone to hear how great you are. You should be paying me for promoting you. You know, like an agent."

Gator doesn't say anything.

I sigh. Never mind profits, it's time for negotiation. "All right, forget the commission. You just round up your boys and be at my house at, say, nine o'clock?"

"You'll have food?"

"Loads."

"Okay, I guess so."

"Great." I give him my address and hang up. I look again at the people I have in my phone, starting from the top. Adora. I think I did a science project with her a couple years ago. Was she the punk goth or the didn't-shave-under-her-arms hippie? Doesn't matter.

"Hello, you have reached Adora's answering device. Imagine yourself free from the conflicts of the world as you leave a message. Enter a new realm of serenity for—"

I hang up and go to the next person. Andre. He's been a bit weird lately. I think he thinks I spread his fake Brent rumor, which I didn't at all since he told me not to. Now I wish what he had told me had really been true. Would serve Tara right.

"Andre, Whitney Blaire. There's a party tonight at my house. Everyone is bringing some food. How 'bout you show up with a pizza?"

Gator's band sucks, but no one seems to care. The party's going full swing as I walk around. People are laughing and dancing, drinking and having a regular grand old time. Good, good for them. Me too.

I picked the lock of Mother's liquor cabinet earlier and poured myself a gin and tonic like I'd seen her do so many times.

It tasted like rubbing alcohol. I drained the first cup and filled it up again, this time adding some maraschino liqueur to it.

I made sure the cabinet locked once I closed it. No sense in letting my whole high school into my parents' good stuff.

Now I'm nursing the second cup. Two gin and tonics and I'm having a ball, a real ball.

"Whitney." David comes up to me holding half a beer and drapes his arm on my shoulder. "This is some party. Did I tell you how great you look?"

I smile. Let him say it however many times he wants. I know it's true. Low-cut shirt and short skirt work wonders. Nice of him to notice, though. I smile some more, giving him the once-over. He's taller than I remember, about an inch taller than me in heels. And he's finally gotten a cool haircut. He has it all gelled and spiked. There's even some stubble on his chin, making him look older. It looks good. He looks good. Damn good.

"So you really think I look great?" I circle my arms around his neck. My fingers trace around his shirt collar.

"Hell yeah!"

"Yeah?" I slide up against him. I tilt my head to the side and look up at him.

He presses against me as he reaches behind me to set the beer down. His arms go around my waist. "Yeah."

I pull him closer. I smell soap and aftershave on his neck as I kiss it. My mouth moves up to his. His arms tighten around me. My fingers dig into his hair. Damn. The boy can kiss!

I run my hands down his chest. There's definitely a nice body under there. A bit scrawny, but there's potential. His hands stay on my bare waist, not letting them wander. I smile in mid-kiss. I know he wants more. I can feel it against my leg.

I pull away slowly. Then I take one of his hands. I start leading him away from the kitchen. He follows. He doesn't say anything. I head up the stairs.

David stops. "Whitney, I—"

I let go of his hand and turn to look at him. "What, you don't want to?"

"Yeah, but—"

"So, come on then." I continue up the stairs. I don't look back to see if he's coming. His loss if he doesn't. I open my bedroom door and go in. A few seconds later I hear the door close. I don't turn on the lamp; there's enough light coming from the window. I can see the shape of him standing there in the middle of my room.

I grab his shirt and pull him toward me. I start kissing him again. My hands tug at his shirt until I pull it over his head. Then I take off mine. His hands suddenly go crazy. Like he's trying to touch everything at once. I chuckle. You'd think he'd never felt up a girl before. Still, it's kind of cute.

And it feels good. It's great to be wanted.

His hands fumble with the bra strap. He can't unhook it. He pulls and twists it but can't undo it. He stops kissing me. Not good. I hear him swear. Then he tries to pull the bra over my chest. I sigh. I reach a hand around and undo it myself. He gets the straps off my shoulders and tosses the bra across the room.

I move him onto the bed. Our other clothes come off. David stops again.

"We can't. I don't have anything."

I roll over to my night table. In the back of the drawer are some condoms I snagged from the school nurse's office. I hand him one.

I keep kissing and touching him as he gets ready. I want this; he can't have any more second thoughts. He doesn't seem to. He's pretty eager but doesn't seem to know quite what to do. I take it in my hand and show him where it goes.

I wince slightly. Everyone says it hurts and it does, but not too bad. It's not great, but it's not bad.

It only takes David a few minutes, then he's done. He lies down next to me, playing with my hair. "Wow. That was great. I love you."

I look up at the ceiling. It's good to have it over with. Through the canopy, I can see the spinning fan. The gin and tonics are wearing off. I hear the music from the party below. I'd forgotten all about it and all the people that are in my house. I don't even think we locked the bedroom door.

"You okay?" David asks. "Was I all right?" He gets up on his elbow and looks at me. In the darkness I can see his silhouette, but I can't really *see* him. I hope it's the same for him.

"Yeah, sure. Perfect," I say.

David starts kissing me again but I push him away.

"I'm going to take a shower. You go back and enjoy the party." I wrap the sheets around me and move quickly to my bathroom on the other side of the room and lock the door.

 *Pinkie*

I'M WAITING FOR ANGELA OUTSIDE A STORE WHEN I SEE
a pair of Converse, a suit, and a messy brown head walking
toward me.

"Nash!"

He looks up and a second later, he has me trapped in a big
hug and is rocking me side to side. "Hey, sorry I had to cancel
this week's meeting. I've been working overtime."

I smile at him. As long as he doesn't kiss me, I can think
straight. "But that's good. Lets you save up money. When do
you think you'll have enough to get to Harvard?"

He runs a hand through his hair, making it stand up more
than normal. "Hopefully, I can go in the fall. I should know by
the end of the year if I'll have enough saved up."

The comment David made about him never having even
applied runs through my head. "So you're all enrolled and
set up?"

Nash makes a sound that means yes. "Just as long as I get
the finances sorted."

"That's really exciting." I'm glad David was wrong. I didn't like thinking that Nash was too insecure to even apply to college. "But then we'll have to get someone else to run the Honor Society."

"Ah." Nash puts his arms around my waist. "But there's still plenty of time. And who knows, maybe the following year you'll be at Harvard too."

My mind races. He's talking about the future, our future! That must mean that we're together, right? Now I just have to get into Harvard. My grades are decent but are they enough? Will I have what it takes to get in? What is it about me that would make my application stand out? I should start working on it now, even though it's still a year away. I have to do everything I can to make it as perfect as possible.

A voice takes me away from my collegiate planning. "Nash!"

We break away. Bursting out of the store, there's Angela. She runs to Nash and throws herself at him. Her legs wrap around his waist as he lifts her up in a hug.

"Look, Nash." She holds up her arm when he sets her down. "I just got these bracelets for my birthday. I'm eleven now, you know."

"No way," he says. "I thought you were thirteen."

Angela flips her hair over her shoulder, a trick I swear she learned from Whitney Blaire. "That's because I'm in the gifted program in school. They're even talking about me skipping sixth grade next year and going straight into junior high."

"No, they're not," I say. Angela gives me a look that says I'm dead for tattling on her. For a second I feel guilty, but then

I remember that I'm the older sister and Nash is *my* pseudo boyfriend, not hers.

But Angela is not about to give up so easily. "Well, they're at least saying that I can take advance classes. I hope they let me take Latin. Do you speak Latin, Nash?"

Nash shakes his head, but keeps smiling. "Only a bit. I took Ancient Greek instead."

Angela's mouth drops.

"Angela, we need to go." Part of me is amused by her behavior, but the other part remembers that in a few years she'll be competition.

Angela frowns. "But I haven't seen Nash in such a long time."

Nash bends a bit to get to Angela's height. "Tell you what. This week I can't, but next weekend I'm completely free. We'll do something then, the three of us."

"Really?" Angela's eyes light up.

"Sure, I'll call your sister later and we'll set something up."

"Cool!" She gives him another hug and then a kiss on the cheek.

Nash straightens up and hugs me.

"You're not really going to call, are you?" I ask softly.

Nash laughs. "Course I am. Don't I always?"

"No," I answer truthfully before realizing I'm being rude.

Nash shakes his head like I'm teasing him. "Sure I do, you silly girl."

He kisses me quickly on the lips. The world doesn't stop turning; my feet stay planted firmly on the ground. I don't even think about our wedding.

Then he waves and walks away.

Angela sighs. "I think I'm in love."

"Get over it," I say in a tone that is more Whitney Blaire than me. "He's never going to call."

"But he promised," Angela whines.

"Well, then keep your fingers crossed but don't hold your breath," I say as I unlock the car. I think about what he said. Unless there's some other Pinkie he phones, he's never called me. Which means he's either delusional or he's a liar. Which are both worse than being a phony. And neither of which is a quality I want in the person I'm dating.

I was happy enough for a while with secret kisses in an empty classroom, but now I want something real, someone who's there for me when I need him. Someone who returns my calls. Or even calls initially. Someone who doesn't lie. And for what Nash has proved, he's a lousy boyfriend.

At the red light, I pull out my phone. Angela is in the backseat staring dreamily out the window. Before I can think about it a bit more and change my mind, I delete his number. If a miracle happens and he does give me a call, let him leave a message with his number on my phone.

 *Tara*

WE GO OVER TO RILEY'S HOUSE AFTER WORKING OUT. Riley reassures me that her parents won't be home until late, though I still don't understand why that should matter. I call Mom to let her know where I am. We make dinner (whole wheat pasta with sun-dried tomatoes, turkey meatballs, Caesar salad, and for dessert Riley brought out organic chocolate-covered cherries) and then we go up to her room. It's the first time I've been there. Her room's as big as Whitney Blaire's, which means half of my house, one whole floor, could fit in her bedroom. But while Whitney Blaire's has white walls and cream carpet, Riley's is more her, with red walls and zebra-striped sheets. Her gymnastics medals take up almost a whole wall.

"I've got lots of trophies too," I say quietly.

Riley turns her head to the side and looks a bit guilty. "I didn't see them."

I sit down on her queen-size bed and stare at my fingernails.

"That's because they're all packed away. From when we moved to our present house five and a half years ago."

Riley sits down next to me looking surprised. "Really? Mine were the first things I unpacked when we moved here."

I shake my head. "That's because you earned yours. Most of mine don't mean anything."

Riley is confused so I continue.

"When I was little and played soccer or softball or any other team sport, everyone got a trophy; whether you won or not didn't matter. One girl sat on the bench reading a book during every practice and game and she still got a trophy because she was 'part of the team.' I told my dad it wasn't fair; only the winners should get something. But he said this way it made everyone feel like a winner."

Riley sympathizes. "But you didn't."

"Of course not," I say, still talking to my hands. "Everyone doesn't win. Not in games, not in real life. I don't think we should pretend for kids. It creates false expectations."

Riley places a hand on my knee. "You're thinking about your dad and what he did to you."

I hadn't realized it, but she's right. I cross my arms over my chest. "Yeah."

She gives my knee a supportive squeeze. "Tell me about it."

So I tell her.

I tell her everything about my dad and how I felt when he left. How I still feel now that I've seen him again. Hurt. Betrayed. Angry. Confused. Unwanted. Indifferent. And despite all of that, how I still wish I could see him more. How I hope that one day I'll actually be able to talk to him and not let my emotions hold my tongue.

I move on to tell her about me and Brent and how I trusted him. A lot of the things I felt with Dad, I felt them again with Brent. I tell Riley how much it hurts what Whitney Blaire did and how I could never forgive her for that.

I tell her all the things that happened before, that are happening now. I never share my thoughts and feelings with anyone, not even with myself. But with Riley it's different. I want to tell her; I want her to know. And it doesn't feel like I'm losing control. While I'm speaking, it's like someone else has taken over my body and is saying things that I'm not aware of. But once they are said and I hear them out loud, I realize they are true. As I tell Riley all about myself, I learn it all myself too.

Through all this, Riley doesn't say much, but I know she's listening to everything I'm telling her. Sometimes she gives me a smile of encouragement or a comforting rub on the knee. When I finally finish, Riley doesn't say anything. She doesn't need to. After all I said, it's good to have the comfort of silence.

With Riley slouched forward, some of her long hair brushes against my hand on the bed. Instead of moving my hand, I look at Riley. The way she's sitting, her hair is covering most of her face. I reach up and move it away so I can see her better. Once I touch her hair, I continue running my fingers through it. It's as thick and soft as it looks. Part of me says I should stop, but I can't pull my hand away. And if anything, Riley doesn't seem to mind. Her eyes are shining at least.

"Your hair is so beautiful," I whisper.

A small smile creeps across Riley's face and her eyes stay looking into mine. My heart pounds in my chest as if I had run eight miles. I don't know what's going on. Part of me suggests I stop, but I can't think of a single reason why I should. Maybe because I can't really think at all. My face gets drawn in closer. I stop myself a few inches from her lips.

"It's okay," she whispers back. Her hand slides up my leg. Like a magnet, I tilt my head and kiss her. Just a light kiss, but right away I notice the difference. Her lips are soft; there's no stubble prickling my face as we kiss. And I know my chin won't be red in a few minutes. Then she kisses me back more passionately. I do the same.

My fingers tangle themselves in her hair, her wonderful, beautiful hair. I can smell her lilac shampoo. My hands go up and down her back. It's so strange. She's so much slighter than Brent; her body feels so different. Softer. Less intimidating. She's still muscular, but at the same time delicate. I feel like I have to protect her, almost like I'm the guy and she's the girl. No. I push those thoughts out of my head. As weird as it is, I want us both to be the girls—no, the women—we are. It's better this way.

My body has never felt like this before. Every part of me Riley touches tingles; every part of her that I touch makes me want to explore even more. I'm like an artist: feeling and admiring perfection. Nothing has ever felt so real and so great. I should know what girls are like, what we feel like, but I can't get enough of Riley's body. Her female body.

One hand moves down to her waist. I can feel a bit of skin where her shirt doesn't reach her pants. I slip my fingers under. I feel her belly ring as I make my way up her shirt. Riley shifts forward, like she wants my hand to keep moving up. I cup her bra. It's squishy from the padding and that just gets me more excited. I want to touch the real things, but I'm scared to at the same time.

Riley takes one hand away from my legs and unhooks her bra through her shirt. Without thinking, my hand slips under the cup and I hold her breast. Wow. It feels great under my hand. I try the other side and that's great too. I have never known why guys are so obsessed with breasts, but now I know. They're fantastic. Soft but firm, they move around in my hands, but stay in the same place. It's so different from touching my own breasts—they just seem to get in the way of the soap when I shower. But Riley's breasts fill my hands perfectly as I play with them. I flick a nipple with my fingers and she moans into my mouth.

Her hands were all over my legs and my butt, but then they move to the button of my pants.

I break away from our kiss and move my hand back down to her waist. I'm out of breath. We stare at each other. Her breath is heavy too.

"Is this okay?" she asks. Her hand stays on my waistband.

I think about her breasts in my hand, the way her hair feels, the way I feel when we touch, when we kiss. My heart is going crazy. This is crazy. We shouldn't be doing this. But I want her. I want her more than I ever wanted Brent. "Yeah. It's perfect. Absolutely perfect."

She smiles as she eases me down onto the bed, and I close my eyes.

Whitney Blaire

MY HEAD IS THROBBING AND THE ROOM FEELS LIKE IT'S shaking. No, not the room. Just me. I open one eye. It's not easy. My contacts are dry and seem to have crusted my eyes shut. I can just make out the orange hair of a bad dye job. I roll over and pull the covers over my head. The shaking continues.

"Go away," I mumble.

"No, no, no. You wake up right now."

"Carmen, please, just leave me alone."

Carmen yanks the covers off. "No. You get out of bed or I bring my spray and get you out."

When I was little, Carmen always sprayed me with a water bottle when I did something wrong, like make a mess after she had just cleaned up. I wouldn't put it past her to still do it. "Okay, fine. I'm getting up."

Carmen watches as I roll myself out of bed. My head still hurts and I can't focus very well. Carmen's eyes stay on the bed. For a second I wonder if I only thought I had gotten out of bed but was really still there. I turn to see if I can see myself sleeping.

Nope, no Whitney Blaire sleeping away her hangover. Instead my eyes land on a blood stain on the ivory sheets.

"Niña, what did you do?"

I lean against the bed post. It's all coming back. The fight with Tara, Mother's note, the party, the gin and tonics, David. As soon as I remember that, I feel the soreness between my legs. "I must have started my period."

"No! You don't start period." Carmen stomps her foot. "You have a party and bring a boy to your room."

I don't say anything. Carmen knows she's right and nothing I say can change that. She knows me too well. I stare at my feet. There seem to be two of them.

Carmen sighs. "Okay, you get dressed and I make you breakfast. Then you help me clean the house. All day we clean. Until the house looks good again."

My fantasy of leaving a mess to make a statement goes out the window. The P.S. on Mother's note that last night I saw as permission now doesn't seem to mean anything. The only thing I want now is for them not to find out. I wouldn't put it past them to sue their underage daughter for misconduct, or subject me to hours of pointless therapy. "You're not going to tell my parents?"

Carmen hesitates. "I don't say nothing if you help me clean. You don't help, then I don't clean and I call them right now."

I lick my lips. "Let me put on some old clothes."

The mess is worse that I thought. I remember going downstairs after I showered. There were people everywhere. Drinking, eating, having a good time. Normally I would have been thrilled to know that I had thrown the party everyone would be talking about. But after being with David, I had just wanted everyone to leave, especially David, who for some reason wanted to stay and help me clean up. I remember screaming very loud. Once I had everyone's attention, I told them to get the hell out. They all listened, even David. Not many people wanted to mess with me. I didn't want to mess with me. Then once they'd all left, I took a few gulps of something someone left and went straight to bed.

And here I am now. Scrubbing a puke stain off the Persian rug. I've already filled the dishwasher twice and taken out the trash a few times. I want to call Pinkie. Try a little Tom Sawyer manipulation to get her to help me out. But it's Sunday. She's doing her little church thing. And there's also the fact that I don't think I invited her to the party. I hadn't wanted her to ruin it. It had ruined itself.

By now David must have asked her why she wasn't at the party. I wonder what else David will tell her. I don't want her to know. On the other hand, I'd like to tell her. But I won't. She won't want to talk to me. Not after I left her out. Not after I did what I did. And I don't want to hear it.

I also want to talk to Tara since she's been through this whole being-with-a-guy thing before. I want the old Tara before Riley came and turned her against me. But the Tara I want to talk to doesn't exist anymore.

I scrub the stain a little harder and hope Carmen is right about club soda.

Tara

I COME DOWNSTAIRS AND SEE MOM WITH HER HAIR loose wearing an old shirt at the kitchen table with her checkbook, a pile of receipts, and the calculator. She's frowning at the numbers. She looks up when she hears me and then glances at the oven clock.

"Good grief Tara, do you feel okay? It's almost eleven o'clock."

"I know," I say, but then look at the clock anyway. "It's just that I have to tell you something."

Mom pushes the papers aside and folds her hands on top of the table. "Okay."

I shift from one foot to the other, then cross my arms and look at her. "I'm seeing someone new."

Mom's head tilts slightly. "And you think I'm not going to approve? Is he a Republican?"

I don't know whether she'll think that or the truth is worse. I take a deep breath. "It's Riley."

Her mouth drops slightly. She blinks a couple times and

then swallows. She runs her hands through her auburn tangles and then stops. Very slowly, she pushes herself away from the table. She fills her mug with more hot water. The tea bag she had left in the bottom half floats and turns the water a pale green. Sound asleep, Sherman snorts from under the table.

"So, what does this mean, Tara?" She swishes the tea around. "Are you gay now?"

I unfold my arms and shove my hands into my shorts pockets. That thought had been going around my mind as well. And I don't know how I feel about it. And I don't know how it changes those disturbing thoughts of Brent and Sanchez that still come to mind. I don't know why images of those two bother me so much. I've tried changing the costar to anyone other than Sanchez with Brent, especially Whitney Blaire. When I think about Whitney Blaire with Brent I'm overcome with fury. When I think about Sanchez with him, I'm disgusted. I wonder if that makes me a hypocrite, especially since I'm with Riley now. But when I think about Riley and what we've done together, I'm overcome with giddiness. The two scenarios are so similar, and yet they make me react so differently.

"I don't know," I answer Mom's question honestly. "But we like each other. Like each other a lot."

Mom drinks half her tea and makes no motion of having burned her tongue. "This is going to take a while to get used to."

"I know. For me too."

Mom nods as she dumps the rest of the tea down the sink. She puts the kettle on again. She throws away the old tea bag and puts a fresh one in the mug. She was drinking Sencha before; now it's Lapsang Souchong.

Rummaging through the cupboard, she pulls out a bag of

cashews. I hear her crunching the nuts as she pops them one by one into her mouth. The kettle whistles and she pours herself a fresh cup of tea. The room fills with the smoky smell as she lets it steep. She wraps her hands around the mug. Steam rises over her face. She takes a few slow sips and then she lowers the mug and finally looks at me.

"Well, the least I can say is that I like Riley better than I liked Brent."

I let out my breath and smile. "Yeah, me too."

"And she makes you happy?" Mom watches me closely.

I smile more. "Yeah, she does. Happier than I've been in a really long time."

Mom drinks some more tea and nods a few times. "Good. Good. Real good. That's the most important thing. And what do your friends say? Have you told them yet?"

My smile disappears. "No, I haven't told them, but by the way they're acting I think they already know."

Mom sets her tea down. "What happened? Is it because of Riley?"

"Yes . . . No. Well, kind of." Just thinking about what Whitney Blaire did to me makes me want to scream. I walk to the back door and then return to the table. It takes two steps each way. I feel myself losing control but at the moment I don't care. "Whitney Blaire is a backstabbing bitch, and I hate myself for hanging out with her for as long as I did. Stupid whore."

Mom doesn't say anything. I don't usually swear, but then again, I don't usually have my best friend seduce my ex-boyfriend.

I go to the cupboard and pull out the chamomile tea. There's just enough hot water left in the kettle to fill my mug.

"I'm sorry to hear you two fell out," Mom finally says. "And what about Pinkie? Or should I not even ask."

I sigh and slightly shake my head. "No, she's fine, I guess. I just needed some space from her and her never-ending worrying for a bit. But now that I'm with Riley, she barely looks at me. Now that I'm gay, or whatever I am."

Mom sets her mug down and looks at me. "It isn't an easy thing to accept. I've always thought I was very open-minded and I'm having a problem getting used to it."

I don't say anything. I know she's right. But at least she's taking this better than Riley's parents, who are in denial, and because of it don't know anything about me yet.

Mom continues. "A lot of other people are going to act strange around you too. Maybe just at first, maybe forever."

"I know, I know all this." I take the bag of nuts and grab a handful. I'm usually not so open about my thoughts and actions, but I need to justify them to Mom, to myself. "But I can't help it. I think I'm in love with Riley. Every part of me is attracted to her. Not just physically, but emotionally and mentally and all those other bits. When I'm with her, everything feels right, and safe. I feel like nothing can go wrong. I've never felt that before. Not with Brent, not with anyone."

Sherman whimpers in his sleep. His nails scratch against the floor as his legs twitch.

"You've been hurt badly by the men in your life," Mom points out. "It's understandable."

I swallow a cashew without chewing it. It scratches my throat, but I manage not to choke. "Do you think Dad and Brent made me gay?"

Mom takes her time answering. Her tea is almost finished. "I don't know, Tara. I just know that you need someone to love and someone you can trust. You haven't found that in men."

This time I chew the cashew until it's butter in my mouth. "I never thought this would happen to me. Riley says she was born gay. But I never liked girls before I met Riley."

Mom reaches over and squeezes my hand. "So maybe you're someone who falls in love with a person, not a gender."

I hadn't thought about that. I always thought people either liked boys or girls. But I was attracted to Riley from the moment I saw her hair floating behind her. I don't know if it would have been the same if she had been a guy. Maybe not. Because some of the things I like about Riley are her female attributes.

The thought of Riley's body makes me blush. It's all so weird and different, but at the same time it doesn't feel wrong. And like I told Mom, Riley makes me happy. And like she said, happiness is a good thing.

I let out a breath and squeeze Mom's hand back. I might not have much of a dad, but I'm lucky to have such an awesome mom.

✒ *Whitney Blaire*

SOMEONE'S CALLING. I SCRAMBLE AROUND MY NIGHT table for my phone. I squint. It's David. Again. He's been calling me so much. This is like the fourth time he's called today. He seems to think we have something to talk about.

But there's nothing to talk about. We both got what we wanted, and he should be happy with that. He shouldn't expect more. I don't.

And yet he keeps calling. I don't know what his problem is, probably just hanging around Pink too much.

Pink's been calling a lot too. I'd like to think David put her up to it, but really, when does Pink need an excuse to use her phone? I've sent her regular text messages, just to let her know I am fine. The last thing I need is for Pink to come over here and break in thinking that I've been kidnapped or something. Then the alarm would go off and I wouldn't want to explain to Father why one of my friends was trying to break into the house.

No, it was easier to send Pink those texts saying I was fine, just suffering from cramps. I still don't know what David told her. I'd like to think Pink would have said something in her messages if she knew. Or maybe she is waiting for me to tell her. Well, she can wait. She's not going to get anything out of me.

The phone stops ringing, but now it's beeping to let me know I have messages. I press some buttons to stop the beeping but ignore the messages. I look at the time on the phone. It's 6:30. I'm not sure if it's A.M. or P.M. The room is just a black hole with the curtains drawn. I can't see a thing.

I blink a couple more times. There it is, 6:31 P.M. That means Mother will be home soon. Which means I need to raid the kitchen before she comes.

As I stand, I realize how hungry I am. I don't know when the last time I ate was. Yesterday? When was yesterday? At the moment I have no clue, but it doesn't matter.

There's nothing to eat in the fridge. Digging around, I find a Corona Light in the back. I pop that open while I look for something else. Some forgotten chocolate caramels are in a drawer. I chew them and keep moving things around. I finally come across low-carb bagels, some lox, no cream cheese. But there is fat-free veggie dip. That works.

Still chewing the caramels.

Then I head to the pantry. Nothing in there either. I rummage around the shelves until I find some microwave popcorn. Perfect.

With the neck of the Corona between my fingers, I hold the plate with the bagel and the rest of the chocolate caramels. In the other hand, I have the bowl of popcorn. I close my bedroom door just as I hear the garage door open. When Mother calls through the intercom that she is home, I tell her I'm busy with my homework. I lower the volume of the TV and eat another caramel.

The phone rings again. Jeez, David. Lay off will you? I'm getting tired of hearing from you. I press NO so that the call goes to voice mail and stops ringing. Thank God. I can't stand that ring tone anymore. I go online and search for a new one. Doesn't matter what it is, just one that doesn't drive me crazy if I hear it a millions times a day. I find one. Some hip-hop boy band I've never heard of. That explains why it's free.

That done, I get back to the TV. At one point Mother's voice reminds me not to stay up too late studying. By three A.M. there's nothing good on anymore. I get my phone and finally listen to the day's messages. David's messages. All five of them.

"Hi Whitney, it's David. Where are you? Call me back, will you?"

I press a button. The robotic voice tells me it's deleted and goes on to the next message.

"It's David again. Hey, are we still on for tonight?"

I turn the phone in my hand then delete the message.

"Whitney, I'm getting worried. Can you please call me?"

No hesitation to delete that one.

"I just talked to Pinkie and she doesn't know where you are. I'm thinking of calling your mom. Are you okay—?"

Delete before he finishes.

"Whitney, I know when I've been forwarded to your voice mail. If this is some kind of sick joke, you suck."

I press the delete button one last time and throw the phone across the room.

I don't know what time it is when I get woken up. At first I think it's David screaming at me, but then I realize it's Mother through the intercom.

"Darling, are you in the bathroom? Can you hear me? I'm leaving now. Is your little friend driving you to school today, or do you need me to take you?" She waits a few seconds and speaks again. "Darling, speak up. I can't hear you."

I roll out of bed and shuffle over to the intercom. Whoever's brilliant idea it was to install the intercom all the way on the other side of the room right next to the door is going to die. I press the button and talk. "Yeah, I'm fine. Pink should be here in a few minutes."

"All right, darling, have fun at school. I'll see you this evening. I shouldn't be too late. Your father is back from San Diego tonight. Don't forget to turn off your curling iron before you go. Did you hear me?"

"Yeah, fine. Bye." I let go of the button and shuffle back to bed. I trip over the phone on the floor. I pick it up and send Pink a text: STL SIK BT DNT WORY C U L8R. Then I pull the covers over my head and go back to sleep.

 *Pinkie*

I LOOK AT THE TEXT MESSAGE FROM WHITNEY BLAIRE
saying that she is still sick. On Monday she sent a text saying
that she was having horrible cramps and couldn't possibly go
to school. It's Thursday now. I swear, that girl has perpetual
cramps. Sometimes I just don't know when to believe her.
I'm pretty sure she was complaining about cramps a week
ago when we had that SAT-prep test. I wish she'd tell me the
truth instead of pretending to be sick. I know something is
going on.

David's been acting funny too. Sunday at church he was
practically jumping out of his skin and had this goofy smile on
his face.

"What's with you?" I had asked.

David smiled impishly to let me know that he knew
something that I didn't. "That was some party last night,
wasn't it?"

I blinked. "What party?"

"Whitney's party."

I remember my eyes widening. "Whitney Blaire had a party last night?"

"Don't you remember? Everyone was there."

I focused hard on folding the program in half. Corner to corner, then running my hand down to make the center seam. "Tara too?"

"I don't think so, but I was too preoccupied to notice."

I grabbed an insert and put it in the program I had folded. I waited for him to elaborate, even though I didn't really want to know. When he didn't, that frustrated me more so I had to ask. "So, you had fun?"

"Yeah!"

"And?"

David got a dreamy look in his eye. "And Whitney and I are dating."

The program fluttered out of my hand. I had to get on my hands and knees to pick it up from under the table. I straightened up and said, "Really?"

David's impish smile grew. "Yeah, I still can't believe it. Whitney Louise Blaire is *my* girlfriend."

I couldn't believe it either.

But I didn't have a chance to ask Whitney Blaire about it since she was sick and didn't want me to pick her up for school on Monday. Or Tuesday. Or Wednesday. Or today.

Then yesterday David called me wondering if I knew where she was. They were supposed to go out and she hadn't shown up. Whitney Blaire has never been known for being on time, and she is forgetful, but she doesn't normally blow people off completely. At the same time, I wonder if this is one of her little stunts for attention. Just like when she got stuck in that tree. I keep thinking what Tara said about Whitney Blaire pretending to have been stuck; if it's true, that stupid thing could have cost her her life.

At any rate, I'm pretty sure she's not suffering from cramps. I wonder if it has to do with the fight with Tara. Must be something big if she thinks giving cramp excuses will get her out of whatever she doesn't want to face.

Normally I'd be worried, thinking that she's ignoring me, but she's not. She's texting me every day so I know whatever is going on, it doesn't have anything to do with me. And it's not like she hasn't done this before. Every once in a while, she just gets in these moods. When she gets this way the best thing is to wait it out until she's ready.

Still, I reply to her text saying: I'M SORRY YOU'RE STILL NOT FEELING WELL. GET BETTER SOON. I MISS YOU! XO. At least this way she knows that I'm thinking of her and really do miss her.

Sigh, but for now it's going to be another lonely day at school.

My phone beeps again and I assume it's her reply. Wrong. It's David. I MISSD THE STUPD BUS. CAN I GET A RIDE?

I turn the car around to head toward his house. Then I turn her around again when I realize I was going in the right direction to start with. He's out the door before I even pull into his driveway. He slams the car door and says, "Let's go."

My worrying radar sends an alert. "What's the matter?"

"Nothing," he lies.

I unbuckle the seat belt and lean over to give him a hug. He pushes me away. "Just drive, will you?"

I reattach the seat belt and shift the car into gear. David

fiddles with the radio, but the stations aren't playing anything he wants to hear. He swears and turns it off. I pretend to look in the side mirror and sneak a glance at him. He's staring out the window, but I bet he's not seeing a thing. I want to hug him. I want him to cry on my shoulder and tell me everything that's wrong. Then I can tell him that everything is going to be okay.

But I don't touch him. I keep talking and acting like everything is okay. At one point I leave my hand between him and the gear shift, hoping he'll take it, but he doesn't. When we get to school, he gets out before I've completely stopped.

"Thanks," he says automatically and then takes off.

I watch him walking away and then roll down the window. "Meet me here after last period and I'll drive you home."

He lifts an arm to wave but doesn't turn around. I don't know if that means that he wants the ride or merely that he heard me.

From the student parking lot, I walk up by myself. Occasionally I wave at someone and say the usual, "hi, how are you, fine thanks," but there's no one I really want to talk to.

By the wall, I see Tara. Her hair is still wet from her morning shower and it's pretty close to freezing. Just seeing that makes me feel colder. I gave Tara a hair dryer a few years ago, and the next thing I knew Whitney Blaire was selling the exact same model of a never-used hair dryer on eBay. I stopped giving Tara beauty supplies after that, but I make sure to give her a nice scarf and natural cough drops every year for Christmas.

I want to go over there and say hi, but we haven't really spoken since she and Whitney Blaire fell out. I've given her mini looks across the hall, but I can't manage much more than that.

Riley is there with her now. I don't have a problem with Riley per se like Whitney Blaire does. But I can't talk to Tara when Riley is sitting on the wall behind her with her arms around Tara's shoulders. It's bad enough thinking of them as a couple, I don't need them to flaunt it. And in public! It's revolting. Small kids walk by the high school and what are they going to think if they see two girls behaving like normal couples do? If Tara and Riley act like that where everyone can see, what's going to keep them from forgetting where they are and actually kissing in public? I don't think I could keep my breakfast down.

Tara notices me. I look away quickly and rush to my first class. I have the textbook, a notebook, and three sharpened pencils out, and my reading glasses on, by the time the bell rings. Every class I share with Tara, I made a point of getting there first and then burying my head in the book so I don't have to make eye contact with her.

At lunch, I eat my BLT with one hand while sorting through my bag to make sure I have all the homework I'd been collecting for Whitney Blaire. At one point Tara walks by me with her canvas lunch bag. I stare at the math sheet I'm looking at so hard, it's like I'm begging the problem to tell me the answer. Once she passes, I watch her sit with some of the other weirdos at school.

Most people seem to accept and ignore the weirdos, though occasionally there might be a bit of name calling. Some people might even avoid being around them, but we're not a school likely to get violent because of them. It's only at lunch when a few congregate at a table that they're intimidating—to me at least; it's their table that usually laughs the loudest. I wonder if they're really saying funny things or just want all the normal people to think they're special. Part of me wants to know why they're laughing. The other part is afraid that everyone might think I'm a weirdo if I go find out.

So instead I go back to my BLT and pretend I belong with the people I'm sitting with.

As I get to my car at the end of the day, I spot David walking toward me from the opposite direction. I smile and give a little wave. He acknowledges me with a slight nod. This time he lets me hug him, but it feels like he's hugging me because he has to, not because he wants to.

"How were classes?" I ask as I unlock the door.

"All right."

I try again. "What do you think about that test we had in poli-sci?"

"I don't know."

One last attempt. "Do you want to tell me what's up?"

"Not really."

And that was it for conversation. I start up the car and we drive off. Just like in the morning, I make small talk, chatting about some teacher or another, but it's clear that David isn't paying attention. I pretend to be cheery and indifferent to his attitude by singing with the radio. He just keeps looking out the window. As I'm about to turn onto David's street, he finally speaks.

"You mind driving around a bit?"

"Where do you want to go?"

"I don't care."

I have to think of something quick since I'm kind of in the middle of the road. It's not a busy road, but still a road. I head toward town. At the very least it'll buy me a couple more minutes before I have to figure out where we should go.

We drive right through the middle of town and once I get to the end, I turn the car around and go back the way we came. I figure we can keep doing that until one of us figures out what we should do or where we should go.

I'm turning around again at the intersection near David's house when he suddenly looks at me. "Are we driving around in circles?"

"More like straight lines."

"Why?"

I want to say because it's more logical to drive in straight lines instead of circles, but I don't want to get him in a worse mood. So I explain: "Because I don't know where to go. So I'm just driving, like you said."

David shakes his head like he's at least a bit amused. "Well then, why don't you drive to some place?"

"Where?" I point in the different directions.

David doesn't look in any of the directions I pointed. "Wherever."

"But where do you want to go?" I insist.

David rests his head in his hands. "Do you always have to be this indecisive?"

I fluster. "I just . . . I want . . . I don't want to do anything that will upset you more."

David closes eyes and shakes his head. "Pinkie, I'm not pissed off at you."

"I know but—"

"So stop worrying," he interrupts.

I fidget some more. "It's just—"

"I mean it," David says while his hand massages his forehead. "Just stop. Or else you *will* piss me off."

I sigh and head to the first place I can think of. We used to go there a lot, but I haven't been since Angela decided she was too old to go to playgrounds.

They added a lot of structures between the time Mama used to take me and the time I would accompany Angela. Originally, there were just two sets of swings, baby swings and big-kid swings, a metal slide that burned my legs on hot days, a merry-go-round that I was always too scared to go on when it went fast, and a sandpit, which was my favorite. Now there are more swings and slides of various shapes, monkey bars, jungle gyms, rope bridges, and all sorts of cooler stuff. When I look at the sandpit now, it just seems extremely unhygienic.

Together, David and I walk to the big-kid swings. I push off and swing low while David just drags his feet in the dirt. I'm about to tell him to stop, that he'll wear out his shoes like that, but I don't want to sound like his mama.

We swing and shuffle for about ten minutes before David finally speaks. "Why's Whitney being such a bitch to me?"

I shake my head. "No idea. I mean, it's not like you've done anything wrong."

David digs his toes into the ground until they're completely covered in dirt. I want to double-check and ask if he *has* done something wrong, but since he's only just started talking to me about what's bothering him, I don't want to shut him up.

"Did she tell you what happened between us?" he asks.

Again I want to ask what did happen, even though I think I have a pretty good idea. My guess is that at the party that I wasn't invited to, Whitney Blaire got caught up in the festive moment and maybe kissed David. David (like I would have) probably thought the kiss meant she was interested in him, but to Whitney Blaire it didn't mean anything.

Instead of asking for confirmation of my theory, I answer David's question. "No, I haven't spoken to her in ages."

David stops digging his hole to China to look at me. "She's not talking to you either?"

The reminder makes me sad and lonely. "I've called her a few times, but she's not answering her phone. She just sends me text messages saying she's not feeling well."

David tries to cover his worry, but I know him too well. "Why, what's wrong with her?"

"She . . ." I stop. I can't discuss menstrual cycles with a boy, even if it is just David. "I don't know exactly. She's not telling me. I think she's just in one of her moods. I think the whole fight with Tara last week really hurt her, unless something else went on that I don't know about. Maybe something with her parents. You know how strange they are."

David goes back to digging the hole, alternating between his heels and toes. Already it's about eight inches deep. Suddenly he jumps to his feet, but then immediately grabs the post as if he's going to faint. "Holy crap!"

I'm at his side in an instant. "What is it? What happened? Are you hurt? Do you need to see a doctor?"

He gasps a couple times before he finally manages to choke out a few words. "I'm fine."

But he doesn't look fine. He's in horrified shock. His eyes are wide open, but I can tell he's not looking at anything. I stay at his side and put an arm around him. This time I don't keep my prying questions to myself.

"Please, David, tell me what's going on."

Slowly he shakes his head no.

I want to insist, but I don't. I tighten my arm around him. "Well, I'm here if you want to talk about it. You just look like you've done something horrendously wrong and the worst thing possible has happened as a result."

David pales and gasps a few more times. "Oh God, I hope not."

Whitney Blaire

I HAVE THE MOST HORRIBLE CRAMPS. I TELL PINK WHEN she calls to see if I'm feeling better. I know she doesn't believe me, but for once it's really true. My gut is killing me, there's a horrible pain in my lower back, I'm sweating like a pig even though I'm freezing, and I barely slept all night because of it.

At first I was glad to get it. I've been having this nasty thought going through the back of my head that maybe I was pregnant. I knew I wasn't. I remember we used something, but there was still that worst-case scenario of "what if." And it didn't help that I was about three days late.

It's Carmen's fault really. The whole day while we cleaned the house, she kept telling me that there was no protection against pregnancy. She went on to say that some cousin's niece's neighbor's ex-girlfriend once got pregnant even though she was on the pill and they used a condom. Someone else while her tubes were tied. Another even though the man had had a vasectomy. And then the last story was a sixty-five-year-old woman who had been through menopause fifteen years before.

That was gross. No one wants to think about nearly seventy-year-old ladies getting lucky at anything other than bingo.

So when I couldn't sleep last night because my stomach was hurting and went to the bathroom just for something to do, it was great to see the blood. Not that I believed all of Carmen's stupid talk, but still, it was good to know for sure that I wasn't. And good to stay home from school another day.

I almost did have to go to school, though. Father's home now and even being on my deathbed isn't good enough to make me miss school. He had wanted me to go when I had chicken pox back in third grade, but Mother reminded him that if I infected the other kids it could end up in a lawsuit. In that case, I stayed home until the doctor signed a form to guarantee I was no longer contagious.

Thankfully, both of my parents left ten minutes before Pink normally comes, so I'm in the clear. It's a big effort considering I want to die, but I called the school as I had done all week pretending to be my mother (I must say, darling, I can do her voice perfectly). The school secretary reassured "Dr. Blaire" once again that "her daughter" was excused. Now there is no way for Father to know that I'm staying home.

I eat some chips left over in the bag by my bed. Fifteen minutes later I'm praying to the porcelain god. Sometime after that, I hear Carmen let herself in and then fuss with the alarm to see why it wasn't on. She finds me a bit later still hugging the toilet.

Instead of being angry, she strokes my head. "*Ay, niña, pobrecita*. You see? I tell you you get pregnant."

I close my eyes and lower my head onto my arms. "No, I'm not."

Carmen puts her hands on her hips. "No? Then you are drunk?"

Even with my head in my arms, the world isn't very stable. "No, really. It's just cramps. The worst cramps ever."

I see her look at the counter where I left the wrapper. Suddenly she crosses herself and says, "*Gracias a dios santo.* We get you to bed, okay? I bring you hot water bag to put on your stomach and you sleep. Later, when you feel better, I bring you some soup, yes?"

She helps me get up. For a second I think I'm going to throw up again, but I don't. Carmen fluffs up the pillows and then tucks me into bed. She's almost at the door when I call her.

"Carmen?"

She turns around. "Yes?"

"*Gracias.*"

She nods and shuts the door behind her.

I wake up when the doorbell rings. I hear Carmen answer it. I can tell it's not Pink or Tara because Carmen doesn't say hello to them. It's a male voice, but I can't tell who it is and what he's saying. Carmen doesn't let him in. I hear the words "sick" and "sleeping." I listen closely but can't make out anything else. The boy says something and the door shuts. Carmen comes up the stairs. She knocks softly on my door and then opens it. I sit up. She enters holding a bouquet of flowers. As she gets closer I see they're roses. Four red ones, one pink, one white, surrounded by those silly little white flowers they put in bouquets.

The card says, *To Whitney.*

David.

I take them and set the vase on my lap. "Thanks, Carmen."

She stands there looking half curious, half surprised, and half upset that a boy brought me flowers. I stare at her. Finally, she takes the hint and leaves the room. I open up the envelope.

Dear Whitney, I'm sorry if I did something wrong. Give me chance to make things right. If I got you into trouble, any trouble, I'm here for you no matter what. Yours always, David.

I read the note again, and again. I swallow, but it doesn't help. Tears roll down my cheeks. The vase tips over on the bed. Everything is wet. The pink rose falls to the carpet and I keep crying.

 *Tara*

I NOW EAT LUNCH WITH A NEW CROWD AT SCHOOL:
Susan (who I think is really a boy trapped in a girl's body) is a
bodybuilder; TJ (whose gender I still haven't figured out and
am too embarrassed to ask) is a swimmer; and Morris, whose
biggest muscle is his tongue. Riley says we should call ourselves
the Gay Athletes Society. I still have a problem calling myself
gay. I'm not ashamed of the relationship I have with Riley.
Every day I'm with her, I'm happier and more in love than I
would have thought possible, but somehow that doesn't justify
gayness in my mind. I still notice the good-looking guys, but
I'm starting to notice the pretty girls a bit now too. I won't say
I'm attracted to them; I just notice them. I notice everyone, but
Riley is the only one I picture naked.

As Mom predicted, I have gotten a few weird looks and
snide remarks (especially in the bathroom or locker room),
some from people I don't even know. On the other hand, there
have also been a couple people who've come up to me privately
and complimented me on "coming out." I don't know how I feel

about that term either. I haven't done anything to justify it. I just don't deny I have a girlfriend.

Riley, my girlfriend. I do like the sound of that. And I guess if that makes me part of the Gay Athletes Society, so be it.

But today there's a new jock invading our table without permission. Chris Sanchez.

What can I say? I don't like Sanchez. Even before the rumor of him and Brent, I found Sanchez vulgar and obnoxious with a tendency to say things just for the shock value. He's not much for morals and doesn't think twice about who he gets off with.

I ignore Sanchez and notice Brent sitting a few tables away. I see him with his new girl all the time now: a dark-haired tennis player I've heard of but have never talked to. I shouldn't be surprised; Brent's not the kind to stay single for long. But it's weird that I haven't seen him with Whitney Blaire. Not even a quick chat. Maybe what they had was just a quick fling. Or maybe it's one of those secret high school romances that no one is supposed to know about.

I'm halfway through my hummus, tabbouleh, and veggie pita sandwich when I hear Sanchez say something to Morris about Brent. Riley, with her hand resting on my leg under the table, is talking to TJ and doesn't notice a thing.

I chew the bite in my mouth slowly. Sanchez keeps on talking to Morris in a hushed voice. "Don't like this new girl of Staple's. She's such a leech. Thank God she's away this weekend. It's been ages."

I stop chewing altogether. The mush stays in my mouth. He's lying. He's showing off. He has to be.

Morris's eyes widen. "Wait. You mean you and . . . ?"

Sanchez makes a shushing motion toward Morris and says in an exaggerated whisper, "Oh, yes, Morris baby. Thought that Andre was going to bust us a while back, but Staple took care of it. Don't go telling anyone, though."

Sanchez dramatically looks around to see if anyone heard him. His eyes land on me with mush still in my mouth. He gasps.

"Oh, no, don't worry, Tara baby," he says, over-apologetic, his face extremely red. "It was like weeks, no, more like months after you two had finished. Really."

I don't say anything. Riley stops talking to TJ and looks from Sanchez to me.

Sanchez keeps on rambling. "Really, I'd never do that. Not to you, Tara baby."

I finally swallow the mush. It feels very solid as it goes down. At one point I think I'm going to choke, but I just keep swallowing.

I put the rest of my lunch away. Riley takes one more bite and crumples her brown bag. I leave the table and Riley follows right behind me.

As I'm walking away, I hear Sanchez frantically telling the table: "Really, you know there was never nothing between me and Staple. Really, I swear. Nothing, never. Because I was just kidding, you know? Staple and me, I just made it up."

I walk by Whitney Blaire. She's back at school after being gone all last week. I glance her way, but she doesn't even notice me. I look at Pinkie. She stares at me for a second, tries to smile, and then sighs before turning away. I keep walking out of the cafeteria.

Riley takes my hand in the near-empty hall. "Tara, I—"

I swallow again as I turn to look down at my girlfriend.

There's only one thing I want to say to her right now. "Did you actually see Whitney Blaire with Brent?"

Riley licks her lips. "No, I didn't. I told you, I just saw her sneaking around the gym."

I can still feel bits of food in my mouth. I keep swallowing to try to get rid of them. "Did you know it was Sanchez?"

Riley shakes her head, her shoulders dropping a bit. "I didn't know anything for sure. Technically, we still don't know."

No, Sanchez didn't actually come out and say he was with Brent that particular day at the gym. But I saw and heard how Sanchez tried to cover up. It's enough to confirm that as much as Brent likes girls, and in his own way maybe even loves the girls he's with, he also likes Sanchez on the side.

Brent with Sanchez, Sanchez with Brent. The images that haunted me suddenly make sense. I see now they didn't bother me because they were about Brent and a guy. I mean, in a way, I'm doing the same thing now. They bothered me because in some subconscious part of my mind, I knew they were real. And it meant that my whole relationship with Brent, my first real relationship, had been fake.

I close my eyes and cover my head. I crumple to the ground until I'm compressed as much as possible. My forehead presses against my biceps while my forearms curl over the top of my head.

I'm suddenly very sure that whoever was with Brent that day in the gym, it wasn't Whitney Blaire. I don't even know how I let myself think she was sleeping with Brent. Maybe I let myself blame her because it was the easy thing to do. Easier to think it was her than to accept the truth about Brent.

"Oh, God. Whitney Blaire," I say, or maybe just think.

A hand rests between my shoulders. Riley places her other hand around my legs. "I'm sorry. I should have never accused her. It was a really stupid thing to do. I'm so sorry."

I don't say anything. I want to stay in my little cave and never come out. But I'm vaguely aware that I'm still in school, crouched against the lockers, where I can still be seen.

"I never meant to hurt you," Riley whispers and tightens her hold. Slowly, I unfold just a bit. Just enough to lower a hand and pick up Riley's. It's dry, but still as strong as it was when we first met. I run my thumb over her fingers, feeling the calluses of her grip.

A little more clearly, I start hearing people walking by and inquiring what's wrong and Riley trying to convince them that I just need to be left alone. Gathering myself up, I get back to my feet. Riley keeps apologizing as she leads me away to a refuge. I keep my eyes shut, but by its location I know that she takes me to the same bathroom where I heard the initial bad news about Brent.

It takes a few more minutes before I get myself together and open my eyes. Riley's tanned face is white with worry and guilt. I take her hand again and hold it to my face. It feels real. But what if the relationship is fake as well? "I'm sorry," Riley repeats.

I bring her hand to my lips and kiss it. I have to believe it is real. Or at least could be.

"Do you think you'll ever tell your parents about me, about us?"

Riley closes her eyes as she brushes her lips over the part of her hand I kissed. Taking a deep breath, she looks up at me. "Yes, I think I need to. They should know I'm in love. But only if there's still something between us left to tell."

"I don't want to lose you," I reassure her. "But I don't want to lose Whitney Blaire either."

Our hands still interlocked, she now kisses my hand. "There's no reason why you should. Not from me, at least."

Riley stands on her toes to kiss me.

I let out a big breath. I don't blame Riley for letting me think Whitney Blaire was in the car with Brent. I blame myself for not realizing that as much as Whitney Blaire flirts, she's never been a boyfriend stealer.

She always reminded me how lucky I was when I started dating Brent. I did wonder why she hadn't gone for him herself, but she said he wasn't right for her. Now I wonder if that was her way of saying she was scared of rejection, and maybe even intimacy. Not going for him and still thinking she could have a chance with him would be better in Whitney Blaire's mind than knowing she didn't have any chance at all.

I remember one time when the three of us were at my house and for some reason Pinkie wasn't there. Brent offered Whitney Blaire a ride home, but she turned him down, saying she wanted to walk. Whitney Blaire hates walking. Only now do I see what she was doing. Or rather wasn't doing. Resisting temptation. And being loyal.

Oh, Tara, says the little voice in my head. *You screwed up big-time and now it might be too late.* I agree with the voice. Whitney Blaire doesn't forgive and forget very easily. I know she acts tough and self-assured to hide her insecurity. And loneliness.

I need to talk to Pinkie. I owe her an apology as well for pushing her aside. I know she'll forgive me. Then maybe she'll help me work on Whitney Blaire. I have to try.

Whitney Blaire

I DON'T SEND DAVID A TEXT UNTIL MONDAY AFTER school. I managed to avoid him throughout the day; I just didn't know what to say. Finally I settle for a simple SORRY.

Instantly he replies: I NEED 2 C U. WE NEED 2 TALK.

I walk the length of my room and back again. I don't really want to see him or talk to him, but I see his point. OK, I reply.

I shower for the second time that day and change my clothes. As I blow-dry my hair I wonder if I should make a big effort and dress to kill, but then think that would be cruel. A little makeup, my favorite worn jeans, boots, and a blue top that Pierre once said brought out my eyes. Just the act of getting ready perks me up a bit, even though I'm not looking forward to what David has to say. With a deep breath, I head out.

We meet at a café that's between our houses. He's already there with his arms crossed. He doesn't hug me. I nod and dump my coat over the chair. He starts to get up, but I wave him away and order the mochas myself: one regular, one skinny with whip. I bring them to the table and use a wooden stick to swirl the chocolate on the whipped cream. David takes a sip of his and then finally speaks.

"Whitney, at the party—"

"I don't want to talk about that," I interrupt. "Look, it just happened and that was that."

David doesn't let it go. "But if there are, um, complications, I—"

I don't know what he's talking about but I guess it has to do with me being out "sick" for a week. "I'm fine. Honestly."

I flash him a smile and hope he doesn't realize it's a fake.

He sits there staring at his drink while I pretend all's well.

"What's going to happen between us?" he asks his drink.

I prepare a surprised look, which he doesn't see. The look then changes to a frown that wasn't prepared. "What do you mean?"

He looks up now, half annoyed, half I don't know what. Confused maybe. "Well, I kind of thought, that you know, after what happened, we'd be a couple. So are we, or not?"

I twirl the wooden stick around in my drink.

David continues. "You've been playing me for years, and that was okay because I thought that maybe, someday, something would happen. And then it did. But then you turned all moody bitch on me. I thought maybe it was because . . . but I guess not. So now, now I don't know where I stand."

David picks up a sugar packet and shakes it so that all the grains fall to the bottom. I know it's my turn to talk, but I don't know what to say. I can't wave it away with a pretend laugh like I might have done another time.

I sigh. "You need someone better than me, David." Now I'm the one speaking to my drink. "You said so yourself. I'm a moody bitch. I'm . . . I don't know. Ask my mother. Scared of commitment or whatever. You deserve someone else."

"I know," he says. I snap up to stare at him. Although I meant was I said, I didn't expect him to agree with me. "But I can't. I—"

I cut him off. "Don't say it."

David bends his sugar packet one way and another. "Don't you like me even a little?"

I take the time to really study him. His hair isn't spiked today, but the haircut still looks okay. He doesn't wear glasses so his eyes are fine. There's a pimple on his chin, but at least it's not gross looking. His teeth are decent. Put together, though, there's just nothing special about him. On there other hand, there isn't anything actually wrong with him either. He's a nice guy. But maybe that's the problem.

"I don't know," I say.

"You were all over me at the party," he mumbles hopefully.

"I was drunk," I answer back, but not as defensive as I might have.

It's a few minutes before David speaks again. "So this is it."

I drain the last of my drink and scrape the side of the glass for any last trace.

Two guys from school walk in. The black guy is in one of my classes and I've always thought he was hot, though I've never talked to him. His friend is pretty cute too, but a bit short. Our eyes meet for a second as they walk by. I look back at my glass, which is still empty, and finally turn back to David.

"I think we should go back to how things used to be and take it from there."

He stops playing with the sugar packet, which is just about to tear in the middle. "So what does that mean?"

"It means we're friends," I say, and then before I can change my mind, I add, "But with the chance that something more might happen."

 *Pinkie*

SOMEONE IS KNOCKING ON MY BEDROOM DOOR.

"Come in, Angela," I say since she's already been in three times. She doesn't believe that Nash hasn't called at all in the last ten days and certainly doesn't believe that I don't have his number. Which is fair enough. I only deleted it from my phone. I know I have the number somewhere else. In fact, I'm sure I could remember it if I tried, but I don't tell her that. I try not to tell myself that either.

I look up from my homework. It's Daddy instead.

"What's that you're doing?" He looks over my shoulder. "Trigonometry? You shouldn't worry about that."

I close the textbook. "Mrs. Bensche hinted that she's going to give us a pop quiz on Monday. I just want to be sure I'm ready."

"It's Tuesday, Mousie," Daddy reminds me. "And you have a four-day weekend coming up. You study too hard. You know, I wouldn't mind seeing you have some fun now and then. Go on a few dates—of course, after we give him a full criminal background check."

"Daddy." I roll my eyes and then wait. I can tell he isn't in my room to chat about my lack of a social life.

Daddy sighs and sits on my bed. "So, Mousie, you know I'm going to Seattle on a business trip first thing Friday morning right?"

"Of course. Barbara's been planning a girls' weekend with Nana, Angela, and me. I heard her talking about egg-yolk masks and mayonnaise conditioner."

Daddy makes a face. "My poor mama, now she'll never go back home. Thank goodness I'll be out of the way."

I grin. Daddy always pretends that he can't stand living with three girls, but I know he loves it. I once caught him watching a girly teen film when he thought we were all asleep. He claimed that he wanted to know how teenagers tick. Which, as far as I'm concerned, shouldn't even apply, because as far as Daddy knows, I've never done anything rebellious in my life.

Daddy's smile leaves his face. "But anyway, I just found out that I'll be gone for more than just the weekend. They want me to go to Tokyo for a week afterward and then give a presentation in New York before coming back home. So I'll be gone about fifteen days."

I don't need to look at a calendar to understand what he isn't saying. I set my reading glasses on the desk and sit down next to him on the bed.

"But Daddy, you can't. You have to be here. You'll have to tell them you have a prior family commitment. You'll miss Mama's . . . I mean, we have to go to . . ."

"Sweetheart, this trip is very important. I can't back out of it."

I push some stuffed animals out of my way. "There has to be something you can do, even if you have to pretend you're dreadfully ill. Or what about your passport? I'm sure it's expired."

Daddy shakes his head. "No, Mousie, I'm going on the trip. And it's okay. You know how much I loved Aurora, and she will always have a special place in my heart. I wish she was still with us, but it's time to let go of her. I have to move on; *we* have to move on. She was a wonderful person, but she's dead."

I pick at the bits of lint stuck to my pajama pants. I think about that day so much, it's like it could have happened yesterday. Yet I doubt I've ever told anyone about it before. "I remember I woke up from my nap and thought Mama was resting like normal when she didn't answer. I thought it was best not to bother her. But the house was so quiet and that scared me. So I turned on the TV and soon forgot all about her. I didn't even check up on her."

Daddy takes me in his arms. I feel like I am four again as I climb into his lap and cry on his shoulder. He brushes the hair from my face and then I feel his chest shaking too. I wrap my arms around him and keep on crying.

"Sweetheart, it's not your fault. Nothing could have been done."

"But if I had called for help, maybe she would have lived longer," I mumble through his shirt sleeve.

"No. It wouldn't have made a difference. When she left, she was gone for good. The best doctors couldn't have brought her back."

"She wasn't supposed to die that day, was she? She did her hungry hippo impression before putting me to bed. We were laughing and she didn't seem sick at all."

He shifts a shoulder to rub against his face. I hold him tighter. "No, I know she wasn't supposed to die that day. She was fine when I left for work, that's why I didn't have a problem leaving you with her. We all thought she had months left. When I saw her there on the bed, it was the most awful moment of my life and I know it must have been the same for you too."

Daddy holds me tighter as he tries to control his crying. "I couldn't believe she was really gone. I was upset that I hadn't been there. I hated that I left that morning not knowing I'd never talk to her again. It was horrible. I was so scared. And I was scared for you too."

The tears slow down and I sniff. "Why? I wasn't sick."

"No, but you weren't even four. I hated that you had to lose your mama so young. And I hated that I couldn't keep you away from all the sickness and then her dying with you in the house. I hated thinking that you had to go through that. I was so scared. Anything could have happened to you being left unsupervised like that. You might have drowned, been poisoned, opened the front door and taken off—you could have done any number of things parents worry about. I realized how close I was to losing you too."

I take his hand and hold it. "I just watched TV. I knew I wasn't supposed to do anything dangerous."

"I know, Mousie. You were born with more common sense than most grown-ups. But you were there. That was more than any child should have to go through."

I straighten up bit, leaning against Daddy. "I'm glad I was there. I don't think I would have understood if Mama had just disappeared. I'm glad I have that last memory of her doing a hungry hippo."

"I'm sure she felt the same way." Daddy rubs my back. "Maybe you don't remember, but when your mama died, she had a smile on her face. She died happy. She always said she'd rather die at home than in a hospital. The doctors wanted her to start treatment again the following week, but she didn't want to. She told me a few days before that it pleased her so much that she could look back on her life and see what a great one it had been. She didn't feel like it had been a waste, short as it was. She loved you so much. She always talked about how lucky she was to have you, so smart, well behaved, and beautiful."

"Daddy, I'm not beautiful."

"But you are. You might not see it, but trust me, everyone else does."

I playfully shove him for being so corny, but I don't make any move toward leaving the security of his lap.

 *Tara*

I'VE BEEN TRYING TO TALK TO WHITNEY BLAIRE FOR THE
last few days. I've barely seen her in the halls, and when I've
called out for her to stop, she hasn't. At lunch I asked to speak
with her, but she continued talking to her friends as if I wasn't
there. Pinkie sat at another table with David and her other
geeky friends. I caught her watching us, but then she sighed
and turned away as usual.

My only choice is to get Whitney Blaire alone. And to do
that, I get to school early the next day and wait for Pinkie to
show up. Fifteen minutes before the bell I hear her car rattling
before I see it. It turns a corner slowly and very carefully parks
between two small cars.

I trot over.

Whitney Blaire is closing the passenger door just as I get
there.

"Whitney Blaire, hold on," I call out to her.

She doesn't turn around. Two strides, I'm at her side and I
take her arm.

She shakes it off. "What?"

"I just want to talk to you for a second."

She gives me her infamous look: a look that makes a person feel smaller than a two-year-old.

"No," she says, and walks away.

I watch for a second.

I look back and see Pinkie biting her lip, staring at us. I need to talk to her too, but I can do that afterward. I don't know when I can get Whitney Blaire alone again. I dash up to her. She ignores me completely. I take a deep breath and start talking anyway.

"Look, Whitney Blaire, I know you're pissed at me and you should be, but I'm really sorry. I should've known you would never hook up with Brent. I was really stupid to think that. If I were you, I wouldn't forgive me either. But it was all a horrible misunderstanding on my part and I should have never said the things I did. I'm so sorry."

I pause for second. She doesn't say anything. She's still walking. I continue. "It's been hard not being your friend these last few weeks. I miss you."

I breathe. She's got to know how hard this is for me. I never express my feelings like that.

Finally Whitney Blaire stops. She folds her arms across her chest and turns to look at me. "So, do you finally believe me that Riley is a backstabbing bitch?"

"That's cold, I can't—"

"Then I can't." She goes over to a group of people, smiles wide, and starts chatting with them as if everything were perfect.

I bury my face in my hands and pull my hair. I stay like that for a few seconds, even though I know at least one person is watching me. I take two deep breaths that come out more like two big sighs. I raise my head, but my eyes stay closed for a second longer.

"Pinkie?"

"Yeah?" she says from behind me. I turn and walk over to her. I want her to give me one of her famous hugs, but I can't move my arms to tell her that's what I want. For a second I think her hugging instinct will take over, but her hands just end up clutching the straps of her backpack.

"I'm sorry. I've been treating you bad too. You didn't do anything wrong. It was just me being, I don't know what. Stupid, I guess. I shouldn't have pushed you away."

"No, you shouldn't have," she agrees. "I know I've always been the odd girl out of the three of us—"

I look down. "That's not true."

She runs her hands up and down her straps, not really looking at me. "It is. And that's okay. But I never thought that if you and Whitney Blaire fell out, that you would dismiss me too."

I shift my backpack to my other shoulder. "I didn't mean for that to happen."

"I know, but it still hurt. You know how much I worry." She now starts fidgeting with her phone.

I close my eyes again for a second. "Sorry. I've missed you too, you know. It's weird coming home and the answering machine being empty because you haven't left any messages." I try to make a joke.

Pinkie doesn't say anything for a few seconds. She presses a few buttons and shows me a screen on her phone. "I did call a couple times but didn't leave a message."

I relax just a bit. As long as Pinkie is still making calls, I know there's hope. "Do you think we can all go back to how things used to be, but with Riley in our group too?"

This time Pinkie really does take forever to reply. The bell rings and we start walking to class. "It's not that easy," she finally says. "I think we all need some time to get used to your new lifestyle."

Whitney Blaire

THE NERVE OF TARA. I DON'T KNOW WHAT SHE'S TALK-
ing about. Saying she forgives me, but she still doesn't see
Riley for what she is. Pink says we don't need to like Riley
to be friends with Tara. But she isn't any better. I don't see
Pink rushing over to hug Riley. And I thought Pink would
hug anyone.

Maybe I should go after Brent. Then she'd really have
something to feel bad about. He's not off-limits now, seeing
that Tara isn't my friend anymore. But there's still that thing
that maybe I'm not *his* type. If I am, I'm not sure I would want
to be with him seriously or for very long. And if I'm not his
type, I don't want to know about it.

I should have pretended to be sick longer. Part of me had
wanted to, but Carmen forced me out of the house. Thank
goodness it's a short week.

When I get home, there's a note on the counter along with
the usual twenty. I don't want to read it. But I do anyway. And
then I wish I hadn't.

Darling,

I'm going to the city to get an early start on Christmas shopping and I might end up spending the night there. Don't worry, I'll be home in time for our Thanksgiving dinner at Le Bon Fromage tomorrow. Your father will be in late tonight. No need to wait up for him, but better not invite your friends over. I'll bring you back a little something.

Yours,

Mother

I scream. It echoes through the empty house. She promised she'd take me shopping in the city next time she went. She promised one day we would stay in a nice hotel just for the fun of it.

So much for promises.

So much for effective parenting.

I take a knife from the block and stab it through the note. It makes a mark on the countertop. I pull it out and thrust the knife in much harder. I leave it sticking out from the counter. I take the twenty and head upstairs.

In one of the spare bedrooms there's a closet with all our suitcases. I grab a small one with wheels. I throw in a few sweaters and shirts, a couple pairs of jeans, a short skirt, my knee-high boots, a hairbrush, my curling iron, my makeup bag with my contacts, some underwear, and the two remaining condoms I stole from the nurse's office.

From the top of my closet, I pull out my secret stash. Years of saving pizza money, birthday money, and every penny I found on the streets has paid off. I have over three grand. I can go anywhere, do anything. And I know my passport is in Mother's office, not locked up in Father's.

I call Pink up. I know how she is and I know if I don't, she'll have the whole Secret Service, or whatever those high-end detectives are called, out looking for me. I'm glad to get her voice mail. I tell her we're going away for the holidays, but will drop a line when I get a chance.

Then I call a cab.

When I'm done I hold on to the phone, looking at it for a bit. Pink sends a text saying to have fun and not do anything stupid. Part of me hopes David would call saying that he and his family are on their way to his grandparents' and would I like to join them.

After a few seconds, I toss the phone in my purse. Not that I would go with David and his snot-nosed family anyway. I have enough money to go shopping in Paris; I could lounge on the beach in Hawaii. I don't need to go on a family road trip.

The cabbie rings the bell. I haul the suitcase off the bed. It thumps down the stairs behind me. I grab my coat and leave the house. I don't set the alarm. And I don't leave a note.

It takes us close to five hours to get to the airport. Everyone and their damn mother is on the road. The cabbie says it's always like this the Wednesday before Thanksgiving. I watch the meter change every few minutes, even though we haven't moved and tell him to go to hell. At one point I think about walking. Then the cab moves a few yards, so I stay. We get to the airport close to nine. I pay the cabbie a shitload of money even though he barely did anything. I could have bought something real nice with what I paid. I stick around to get my twenty cents change.

The airport is packed. The lines to the ticket counter are

longer than I've ever seen them. I go to the airline my parents always use.

It takes forever to get to the head of the line, but finally I'm there. The man behind the desk is in his forties and looks like he's about to die of boredom.

"Where are you flying to?" he asks without looking up.

"I'm not sure. Can you give me a price comparison between Paris and Hawaii? Oh, and maybe Thailand too. Just wherever, really."

Now the man does look at me. I bat my eyelashes and smile sweetly.

"What dates?" he gruffs.

I force myself to stay smiling and pretend to flirt. "Silly. Today of course."

"There aren't any flights today."

"What?" I lose the smile.

"We only have three fights left tonight: St. Louis, Phoenix, and Tallahassee. St. Louis leaves in fifteen minutes, so you won't make it, and Phoenix is sold out, so it looks like Tallahassee."

I drop the charming act and demand. "What the hell am I going to do in Tallahassee? Can I get a connecting flight somewhere else from there?"

"Not tonight."

I think for a second. Tallahassee is in Florida, I think. Which means it's close to Disney World and Miami Beach. "Fine, I'll go to Tallahassee."

The man types in some numbers. "When are you coming back?"

"I don't care, a few days, a week, whatever."

He types some more and then speaks. "That's one thousand—"

"One thousand! You've got to be kidding!"

The person waiting next in line calls out, "Hurry up, missy. Some of us don't have all night."

I try to smile again at the airline man. "I don't need first-class tickets."

"These are standard coach seats."

I try one last time since I'm obviously not connecting with him. "I'm sorry, could you repeat the price?"

He says it again, and still I don't hear anything after a thousand. I could do it. I have enough. But if it's that much to fly somewhere, how much is everything else going to cost? Between the flight and what I already paid the stupid cabbie, I wouldn't be left with much. Probably not enough for a few nights in a hotel, food, and a taxi to get to Disney World and Miami Beach. And not to mention any money left for shopping.

"I think I'll try another airline," I say as I gather up my bags.

The man shrugs and then says, "It's the busiest flying day of the year and you're booking at the very last minute. You're not going to find anything cheaper." And then he waves to the next person in line.

I shuffle out of the way. I can't even pretend that it's his loss. I walk over to the monitors listing all the flights. I have to blink a few times to read what they say. There's just a handful, and none of them is going anywhere fun. Tomorrow's flights aren't up there yet. And I don't want to go back and ask the airline man what they'll be.

I close my eyes and count to ten. When I open them, there's one less flight on the screen. I stay there for a while longer until someone comes by with a mop bucket. I wheel my bag to the nearest chair and plop down.

The crowd is thinning. I wonder how long before everyone is gone. I wonder if there's a time they make everyone leave.

A scruffy man sits down two seats away from me. He takes off his shoes and stretches out his legs. Then he picks his nose. He wipes his finger clean under the chair and goes back to picking his nose. He looks up to see me watching him and winks.

I get up and move away.

I feel his eyes on me while I duck through the remaining people. I head to the other side of the terminal. Even then, I feel his eyes searching.

I can't do this. I can't spend the night in the airport. I can't fly to some random place and not know what I'm doing there. As much as I want to get away, I can't. I'm scared.

I think about calling Pink to come get me. But then I remember how slow she drives, how she always manages to get lost—chances are I'd be waiting for her till Christmas.

I wish Tara could drive. She knows how to get where she's going. She'd pick me up, if she knew how to drive. And if we were still friends.

I let out a sigh. I don't want to pretend anymore.

I want to go home, but I don't want to go to my house. But I don't see any other choice. There's no one else I can turn to. I pull out my phone and scroll down the phonebook.

She answers on the third ring. "'Ello?"

I take a deep breath. "Hi, it's me. I'm at the airport. I'm—I don't want to be here. Can you come get me?"

"Why are you at the airport? You're crazy."

I see the scruffy guy shuffling to the bathroom. He stops for a few seconds to scratch his ass.

I turn away so I don't have to watch, but then check to make sure he's not coming up behind me. I don't see him, but that doesn't make me feel better. I clutch the phone and whisper, "Just come get me. I'm all by myself. Please, Carmen, hurry."

 *Pinkie*

THIRTEEN YEARS AGO TODAY, ON NOVEMBER THIRTIETH, my mama died at home. I saw Daddy crying on her chest and she didn't move. Strange men covered her up and took her away. I wasn't quite four years old, and yet I remember everything about it. Right down to the pink sweatpants and daisy sweatshirt she was wearing.

I remember thinking she looked like a fairy princess, like Snow White sound asleep. I remember telling Daddy that all he needed to do was kiss her and she'd wake up. Yet even with all that wishful thinking, I still knew deep down what it meant when someone died.

I've always known that she would never come back, but I've always been determined to keep her from ever really going. That's why I started writing letters to her. At first they were drawings with my name and "I love you" scribbled over them. Then, as my writing got better, so did the letters. Everything that happened, everything I didn't understand, that I wanted to talk about with someone but didn't want anyone to know about, I put in the letters. Some people write in their diary; I wrote to my mama.

She was my best friend when Tara and Whitney Blaire, not knowingly, made me feel left out. She was my enemy when I couldn't handle her not being there for me. Whatever or whoever I need her to be, that was Mama.

And today is the day she died, thirteen years ago.

Every year, Daddy and I plan a special surprise for Mama: cards, flowers, candles. We bring poems, stories, comics, and newspaper articles that we think she might like, and spend hours reading them to her. There'd be photographs to share and report cards show off. One year, the year we went to Barbara's parents' house for Thanksgiving, we brought Mama some leftovers. Every year we do something. It's a tradition. It's the only time when just the three of us are together again. Our own family.

But now, for the first time in thirteen years, Daddy isn't going to be there. He didn't even leave her a card or ask me to pick up some flowers on his behalf (though I did anyway). I feel like he's betraying us. I also feel that if he really wanted to, he could have been here. For Mama, for both of us.

I planned to go straight after school, but I forgot the scented candles at home. It's okay, I tell myself; it'll only take a couple minutes to stop by and pick them up.

It's pouring when I get home. Lightning, thunder, and pelting raindrops. It has never rained before on Mama's day. I can only hope that it'll stop soon. I go in to get the candles and run back to the car. She doesn't start. I try again. Nothing. I speak to her nicely and tell her I'll get her oil changed 100 miles before the next 3,000-mile deadline. Still nothing.

I sit in the car for a few minutes wondering what to do while the rain continues. It's too far to walk, I haven't ridden a bike in so long I've probably forgotten how to, there aren't any buses that go from my house to the cemetery, and even if I knew how to ride one, I don't have a horse. I put my head on the steering wheel and pray for a miracle.

I hear tapping on the window and I scream. Through the rain, I make out a giant wearing a raincoat and holding an umbrella. Oh, thank goodness, it's only Barbara. Still, I make sure there's no hook in her hand before rolling down the window, just in case.

"The car won't start," I say.

She nods over to her minivan. "Come on. I'll take you."

I gather the bags and run over to her car. The sliding door is open and I jump in it. I set the bags in the back, then squish my way to the front. We buckle up and head for the cemetery.

The rain hasn't stopped by the time we get there. I take a deep breath.

Barbara turns off the car and pulls out a magazine. "I'll wait for you here, unless you want me to come with you."

"No, that's okay."

"All right. Take your time, but if you're going to be longer than twenty minutes in this weather, I want you to give me a call, just to make sure you're not frozen or something."

I smile. "Don't worry. I'll be careful."

I grab the bags and leave. Normally, Daddy and I spend hours with Mama, but Barbara is right; it's too wet and cold to stay very long.

Right away I realize there was no point in stopping home

for the candles; I forgot the matches. And the bits of paper I brought to read to her get soaked through before I finish unfolding them. I made a wreath of flowers to put over the headstone like a tiara, but within seconds the rain tears it apart.

With nothing left to do, I crouch down and speak to her as freezing water pours down my face. "Hi, Mama, it's me Pinkie. Daddy couldn't make it this year. He's in Japan for work, which is about as far away as he can get from being here. He hasn't been gone more than a few days, but I really miss him. I think it's just this time of year that seems so lonely. Even when Daddy was here, I've been feeling very left out. Whitney Blaire has been very hot and cold with everyone lately. Even when she laughs I can tell she's just pretending. I told her she seemed depressed and she agreed. But when I told her she should get help she said no, that she was happy being depressed. I don't understand.

"As for Tara, I don't know if we're friends. It's really awkward being around her. I don't know what to say or do. I want to give her a hug, but I just can't. I can't. I can't be myself around her. I want to gossip about cute guys, but I can't. I want to ask her what she thinks of my new top, but then she'll notice my body so I can't. I can't act normal around her anymore."

I move a lock of wet hair from my face. Rain has poured around my collar and soaked my raincoat through. I start to shiver.

"But at the same time, I don't want to lose Tara's friendship, or Whitney Blaire's. We have so much history; I don't want it to end. But I've also figured out that they can't be my only good friends. David is great, like a brother. Trina in trigonometry seems nice. And there's this funny-looking guy, Oliver, I'd like to get to know now that he's called me back about some poli-sci homework.

"So I'm not forgetting my old friends, nothing like that, but after these last few weeks, I know my childhood friends can't be my only friends."

I jump as a loud clap of thunder seems to shake the earth.

"Okay, Mama. I'm freezing and if I don't get back soon, Barbara's going to send those rescue dogs with the alcohol barrel around their necks to come after me. I'm sorry I couldn't make this a better party for you, but I'll come again soon. Remember I love and miss you."

I blow a kiss her way, grab the bags I came with, and stand up. My legs are all cramped up from being crouched down. I walk stiffly back to the car. Once again Barbara opens the sliding door for me.

"Here, take off your wet clothes and set them on the floor," she says.

The car is all steamed up from the heater and the humidity. Barbara hands me a sweatshirt that goes down to almost my knees. Then turning around in her seat, which can't be easy considering she's well over six feet and over two hundred pounds, she wraps the picnic blanket that lives in her van around my shoulders. It drapes down to my ankles. Dry grass and other debris scratch my legs, but I tell myself it's part of the insulation.

I squeeze up to the front seat.

"Better?" she asks as she fastens the seat belt for me.

I pull the blanket around tighter. "Yeah, thanks a lot."

"Should I drive by and get us some hot chocolates to go?" she asks as she starts the van.

"Yes please, that'll be great." I shift a bit so the seat belt isn't holding me prisoner. "And thanks for driving me to see Mama. I couldn't not see her."

"I know how important she is to you."

"You're important to me too," I say to Barbara before I realize what I said. I look down, pick bits from the blanket, but still I know that Barbara glances at me for as long as possible while driving. At the traffic light, she shifts the minivan into park and leans over to kiss my forehead.

"As far as I'm concerned, you're as much my daughter as Angela is. I've raised you."

She's right, though I've never wanted to think about it. While Mama gave birth to me, Barbara has been my real mom. As much as I wrote to Mama for comfort, Barbara was the one who always came to my rescue. She was the one who really was there for me when I needed her. She was the one who held my hand the first time I was getting a cavity filled. She was the one who picked me up from school in fourth grade because I had stained my pants. She was the one who answered honestly when I asked what it's like to have sex (at least I hope she was being honest). There are so many awful people Daddy could have married; it's good he found Barbara. All these years I've been missing a mama without realizing that I at least had a mom.

What I told Mama about needing to have more close friends than just Tara and Whitney Blaire suddenly hits home.

Just because I had a mama, it didn't mean that I couldn't also have a mom. I remember what Daddy said about having to move on. Maybe he's right.

A few hours later, after we had gotten home and I had taken a long hot bath, I get started on my homework. I come across a problem that is giving me some trouble, so I pick up the phone. It rings two and a half times before he picks it up.

"Hi, David," I say. "It's me, Adriana. Adriana D. Ricci."

 *Tara*

I'M UP HALF THE NIGHT, EVEN THOUGH I WENT TO BED
early. Half of it is nerves and the other half is adrenaline. And
then there's my mind traveling at light speed thinking about
everything that has happened in the last couple of months. By
the time five o'clock rolls around, I'm glad just for an excuse to
finally get out of bed and stop thinking.

Last night I tried one last time to get through to Whitney
Blaire. I called her up to remind her about the marathon and
let her know that I would like it if she was there, even if it
was just for the end. I just hope she doesn't delete the message
without listening to it first.

I also left a similar message on Pinkie's phone inviting her to
the race. I begged her to see if she could get Whitney Blaire to join
her, and then told her I'd drop off a copy of the map first thing in
the morning so she wouldn't get lost. If she decides to come.

For breakfast I have almond butter on multi-seed bread
with a glass of grapefruit juice. I look over my shoes to make
sure they're still fit and sound for twenty-six miles. Before

slipping them on, I take the half twenty-dollar bill and place it in the bottom of one of the shoes for good luck.

We leave at seven: Mom, Riley, and me. Sherman gives us a sad look when we don't include him. The drive takes us about an hour. I eat a banana along the way and drink some water. The roads are still open, but already the traffic is building up. After parking, we head over to registration. By nine I'm all ready and still have an hour to wait. At nine thirty they start lining us up. All eight and a half thousand of us.

We're divided into two groups: the elite athletes (or rather the ones who expect to finish) and those who are running (or walking) for the fun of it. Most people are wearing T-shirts with the charity they're running for on them. I don't see anyone with my shirt, but then again they're only a small local organization that gives support to single moms. Some people are wearing homemade T-shirts with funny slogans, or Halloween costumes. Among the distinguishable ones, I've seen Spider-Mans (one might have been Spider-Woman, but I'm not sure), Supermans, Power Rangers in every color possible, Dracula, Cinderella, Elvis, a male cow, and two people within the same chicken costume.

I decide my goal, other than running the twenty-six miles in about four hours, is not to let the two-headed chicken beat me.

At ten o'clock the whistle blows. Thousands of people take off. A few pace setters break into the front, following the car that is leading the way. I think of dog racing where the greyhounds chase after a mechanical rabbit.

I want to break free from the pack. Even though I started in the elite group, there's still this horrible mob for the first few miles. I know my pace and if I increase my speed so early in the race, I don't know if I can finish it. I grin and bear it, even though it's very claustrophobic. I inch my way to the edge of the road and at least it's a bit better there.

By around the fifth mile, people are slowing down. The Pink Panther is on his back and Mighty Mouse is sitting on the sidelines. Me, I'm just warming up. I squirt some water into my mouth and lengthen my stride just a bit as the road becomes clearer.

I pause to top off my water at the nine-mile checkpoint. I pour in a packet of Emergen-C. It's still fizzing when I drink some. Not too much. Just a sip. Any more will only cause a stitch in my side. I'm back on the course in less than a minute.

By mile marker seventeen, I'm starting to feel tired. I stop in the Porta-Potties. I don't have to go, but this way it doesn't feel like I'm taking a real break. I see someone in costume up ahead. I open a Clif Bar and nibble on it while I keep running.

At mile twenty-two, I'm certain I can't go any farther. My lungs feel hollow and my heart can't beat fast enough to make up for the exertion. My legs feel like they will fall right off. Even my arms are sore. I look down at my shirt. I wonder if the sponsorship I collected is conditional on finishing the race. I can't let them down, but I don't know how I can finish. I'm running alone now, though I can see other runners not too far ahead. I think about waiting for a group to come by just to join them, so we can motivate one another. My stride shortens a bit.

But then I hear the crowd cheering and clapping. There's no one for yards around. They're cheering at me. I notice a tall girl in high heels and a miniskirt.

"C'mon, blondie!" she screams. "Show us that girl power. Don't give up now. You can do it!"

I give her a quick thumbs-up and she cheers more. My legs extend a bit longer. More and more people I don't know call out to keep going. They clap and cheer and wave banners that say GO FOR IT! and MAKE US PROUD! and YOU ROCK! as I pass. All these people say I can do it and I start believing them. I don't know how, but I will do it. I can't let them down. However long it takes me doesn't matter. I'm not competing with others. I'm just competing against myself. Just as long as I do it, I win.

The boost from the crowd keeps me going like a steady hum. By the time I hit the twenty-fourth marker, I'm on autopilot. I can't feel my legs, my heart feels like it's beaten out of my chest, my lungs burn, and yet it seems like something is just keeping my body moving without me having to do anything other than go along for the ride.

At twenty-five, it's insane. I find this burst of energy I must have hidden in some unknown part of myself. I increase my speed and the crowd goes wild. People are screaming things like *1000, 900, 800.* When they get to *700,* I figure out they're screaming the yards. Yards! No more miles, I'm on the homestretch. I hear *400* up ahead. I pass that point. The crowd is so loud now that I can't hear what anyone is saying. I just hear the noise that seems to say, *Go! Go! Go!* I see the posts at the finish. A big clock marks the time. I'm there, five more seconds, and I did it. The screen flashes 3:54:18 as I run by.

I am more tired than I've ever been in my whole life, yet knowing that I actually did it gives me enough adrenaline to cool down appropriately: walking, stretching, and drinking sips. Someone comes to collect my time chip and someone else hands me a bottle of Gatorade. Race stewards wave to move on and clear the area. A couple of paramedics carry a runner to the first-aid tent. I take this all in as I look around for Mom and Riley. We said we'd meet by the green massage-therapy tent, but we didn't think of the thousands of people lurking about. I make my way around the tent, careful not to leave any body part behind.

I see Riley's hair flying behind her before I see her running to me. I lift her off the ground and spin her around, even though I can barely hold myself up. We kiss quickly and then I let go to hug Mom, who looks like she's going to cry. A couple instructors I know from the gym come over and give me a pat on the back. All around people I don't know cheer and congratulate me. Someone reminds me to pick up a marathon T-shirt and a souvenir water bottle. The crowd gets thicker as more people finish the race and more and more spectators come to congratulate us.

I almost don't see her, but standing to one side is Pinkie. Even though I just ran 26.2 miles in four hours, I jog over to her side. She looks nervous and out of place. I take her in a big hug and am glad that she hugs me back. She breaks away quickly, but I'm happy enough with something that resembles the old Pinkie.

"You were fantastic. I could never do that," she says.

"Thanks, but you do so many things I could never do," I answer back.

She blushes and looks down. Her phone beeps and she quickly checks it. I look back at the rest of the people there supporting me. It's good to see them all here.

"Tara." Pinkie holds out her phone. "Here, I'll replay it for you."

I take the phone and listen to the message. It's from Whitney Blaire. "Pink, what's all this Adriana shit? No, David, I don't think it suits her, she'll always be Pink to us. Anyway, tell Tara we saw her on TV. Tell her . . . tell her she did real good. And . . . yeah. Okay, David's here waiting for me. Catch ya later."

I flip the phone closed and hand it back to Pinkie. As unlike me as it is, I give her another hug. This time she doesn't break away. I squeeze her hard and then let go. "Thanks for being the glue that keeps us together. I'm really lucky to have you as one of my best friends."

We walk back to my friends and family who came to watch me run. Although I hadn't noticed it while running, I'm suddenly conscious of the half twenty in my shoe. Everyone that matters is here in some form or another, or at least saw me on television, which is just as good.

More people congratulate me, patting me on the back or shaking my hand. Two little girls ask for my autograph. I smile and tell them to keep it safe in case it's worth something later on. I drink some more water and pour a bit over my head. Pinkie says something about catching pneumonia. I smile but ignore her just the same. Mom hands me another Clif Bar and some orange juice. I down them quickly, realizing how starving I am. Someone from the gym suggests we go for some food. My stomach rumbles as I think about chicken with brown rice and steamed veggies. Or a bacon cheeseburger. But with organic meat on a whole wheat bun. Yeah. And chocolate cake. Dark, fair-trade chocolate.

My stomach moves my legs toward the car. Riley puts her arm around my waist, and Pinkie doesn't look away.

ACKNOWLEDGMENTS

A big, heart-filled thanks to Sarah for seeing what this could become, and to Elizabeth and everyone at Egmont for making it become what it is.

Thanks to Heather for tips on training and running a marathon, and to Bianca for gymnastics tidbits.

Special thanks to my friends and tutors at Bath Spa who helped greatly at its early stages. Had they not been there, the story would be very different.

And big hugs to my family and friends, particularly the Noonans, Waldens, and Lovett-Marianos, who feel like both. Without everyone's love and support in past years, I wouldn't have gotten this far.

ALEXANDRA DIAZ grew up in a bilingual Spanish/English-speaking family, where she started creating stories before she could write, and didn't stop once she could. She's lived in Puerto Rico, Austria, the United States, and Great Britain. *Of All the Stupid Things* is her first novel.